Rush

Also by Nyrae Dawn

Masquerade

Façade

Charade

Rush

NYRAE DAWN

New York Boston

Forever
Hachette Book Group
237 Park Avenue, New York, NY 10017
Hachettebookgroup.com
Twitter.com/foreverromance

First ebook and print on demand edition: May 2014

Forever is an imprint of Grand Central Publishing.
The Forever name and logo are trademarks of Hachette Book Group, Inc.

The publisher is not responsible for websites (or their content) that are not owned by the publisher.

The Hachette Speakers Bureau provides a wide range of authors for speaking events. To find out more, go to www.hachettespeakersbureau.com or call (866) 376-6591.

ISBN 978-1-4555-8237-2 (ebook edition)
ISBN 978-1-4555-8365-2 (print on demand edition)

This book is dedicated to everyone who's had to fight for the right to love equally. To anyone who's ever questioned how they feel or who they are. You're exactly who you're supposed to be, and that is a beautiful thing. Love is a beautiful thing. Love always wins.

Acknowledgments

My husband and children always have my back. They're the reason I'm able to do what I do, and I thank them for their support. Thanks to the rest of my family as well. To my awesome editor Latoya who loves Alec and Brandon like I do. To my agent, Jane. As always, you're a rock star. Thank you for everything you do for me. DJ, Jolene, Julie, Elisabeth, thank you for your insight. Thanks for reading Alec and Brandon's story and opening your hearts to my boys. And to my readers. I think I'm probably the luckiest author in the world. Your support means the world to me and I hope you love Alec and Brandon's journey.

Rush

Prologue

Brandon

October

After a really hard football game, my body always aches. Sometimes the pain in my muscles is dull, sometimes sharp. I have to wrap a wrist here, ice a back there. Sometimes it doesn't faze me and I'm out with the guys, other times I'm laid up.

Every single time I feel any kind of ache, it's always after one of my favorite football games. There's something to be said for ramming into another player so hard, or running with such intensity that your body feels the effects of it afterward.

My whole life, that's how I defined myself. When I was on the field or sore from a game I felt like me—the Brandon everyone knew. The guy who loves football more than anything. The one who's good as hell at it.

The summer after I turned sixteen, I discovered a new side of who I am. It was scary because this me was realer than any other version of myself. It was the Brandon I had never admitted existed.

It hid inside me, afraid and fucking weak and trying to blend into the shadows, hoping, praying to disappear.

Here, that Brandon worked his way through the maze and all that darkness to find its way to the surface. No...I can't even say it was *here*. Lakeland Village, Virginia, isn't what lured that secret Brandon out of hiding. It was *him*.

It was Alec.

The sound of wheels on rocks pulls me out of my thoughts.

Alec's truck drives into the gravel turnout, hidden by the trees. As soon as it does, I don't wait for him. I start to walk a little ways into the woods, to this place we started going to our third summer together as teens. *Together? We were never really* together. *It's not who I am.*

"What are you doing here, man? Why aren't you at school? You should be in Ohio." Alec steps up next to me. I stop walking and he stares, cocks his head a little, his hand going through his blond hair.

"How's school going for you?" I ask, needing to talk, but not ready to do what I came to Virginia to do.

Alec shrugs. "I don't know. It's school, I guess. I'm a freshman at some nothing community college. How's it supposed to be?"

"You should be playing ball," I tell him. Alec shakes his head instead of arguing. He never tried to leave this place. Even when his best friend Charlotte moved to New York to be with my brother Nate, Alec never pretended he planned to leave Lakeland Village.

"Where would I go?" he asks. "I'm not like Charlie. I never had dreams to follow that took me out of here. I'm good at football, but I'm not as good as you. There weren't scholarships for me."

You could come with me. We could be together.

Stop! Man the fuck up, Brandon!

I didn't come here to get Alec to go with me. He would if I asked, though. I know that. Even though no one except Charlotte and Nate know he's gay, he'd go. Despite the fact that his asshole dad would disown him, he'd want to be with me.

He's a year younger, but a hell of a lot stronger than me.

Taking a step backward, I almost stumble, but then my back comes in contact with a tree. I lean against it, cross my arms, and feel that pain, that ache I get after a hard football game.

Only this time, it's nowhere except my chest, and I don't welcome it.

"You're being weird. What are you doing here, Brand?"

My eyes fall closed. I'm not strong enough to be with him, but can't handle walking away either.

"Hey…what's wrong?"

I open my eyes and Alec's walking closer to me. He grabs my waist, stands between my legs, and looks at me. Fucking A, my eyes start to sting and I'm scared I'm going to cry or something.

That's when I see the switch in him. The smile slowly eases off his face. His dark blue eyes storm over and he tenses against me.

He knows.

Unfolding my arms, I slide one of my hands behind his head, through his hair, while the other latches on to his waist. "Come here." I pull Alec into my arms, his face in my neck, while I squeeze him as tightly as I can in this hidden area of trees.

My grip is so fierce, I wonder if I'm hurting him. It doesn't make me ease up. He doesn't either as his fingers dig into my sides.

We don't talk, just hold each other, both of us probably knowing this day would come anyway. What's the point in torturing ourselves if we can't make it real?

My heart spikes when Alec leans back. I think he's going to

walk away and the urge to hold him tighter slams into me, but he just puts his forehead against mine.

I slide my hand down to the back of his neck, fisting it there, and wonder what the fuck is so wrong with feeling like this. With holding him like this and having someone who knows you in ways you're too afraid to admit to yourself.

Or at least why I can't be brave enough not to give a shit what my team would think about it.

"I don't even know who I am," I whisper, closing my eyes. Which one is the real Brandon? The college football star? The shit-talker? The one who's dated girls he's not interested in? Or the one who's with Alec right now? The one who hid away with him and talked to him for the past four years?

"And I do? I listen to my dad talk about queers and I laugh like it's funny and then I sneak away to call you. It doesn't matter. We know who we are together."

His lips brush mine, sending an electric current through me so intense, I jerk back. If I don't, I won't be able to walk away. I won't want it to end.

Alec flinches like I hit him.

"It's too fucking hard. I don't want to be all these different versions of me. I don't want to be scared someone's going to find out and then worry I'm eyeing them in the locker room. I play college ball, man. I want…" *Not to be confused, or scared or worried about what someone thinks of me.* For a second, I let myself study the light trail of stubble on his face. See the cut of his muscles showing under his shirt, before I look down. "I could go to the NFL one day."

"You're a sophomore. We don't have to rush."

This time it's me putting my hands through my hair. I latch on, trying to make sense of the thoughts that are a whirlwind even in my own head. "I don't want to fake it anymore. The guys talk shit when I don't hook up, and when I do, I feel guilty."

Alec's eyes slant, his stare going hard. "I never made you feel guilty. Maybe it's not guilt, but the fact that it's a lie."

"And you're so much better? Your whole life you planned to marry Charlotte."

"That ended over a year ago! I've been honest with myself since then."

"No, you knew you lost her to Nate and didn't have a choice!" My body's tight, my breathing heavy. My mind keeps repeating, *Shut up. He's the only person who really knows you. Who understands everything he sees when he looks at you.*

But right now…he's looking at me like I'm a stranger. "Fuck you, Brandon."

He turns to walk away, but instinct makes me reach out and grab his arm, to stop him. "I want things to be easy. I don't wanna be different, Alec, and I don't want to hide calls to you and pretend things are going to magically change. It's so fucking hard to be all these different people. Maybe it's just you. I mean, I felt attracted, but I never touched any other guy until it was you. Maybe…maybe if I don't always have you in my mind all the time, I can move on."

The second the words are out of my mouth, I know they're stupid. I'm in conflict with myself. My head knows they're a lie, but my heart's begging them to be truth.

Alec's eyes cut through me, his jaw tight. I don't see his fist coming until it's too late. It connects with the side of my face, making me stumble backward. I taste blood in my mouth as my hand comes up to cup my face. As crazy as it sounds, I'm almost thankful he's mad. Hopefully, that it will make this easier on him.

"Maybe that'll take me out of your head. Good luck being straight now."

Alec walks away—that pain in my chest threatening to break me apart. To break me in half. It didn't come from working hard on the field or from being who I'm supposed to be. It came from running like a fucking coward, and there's no going back.

Chapter 1

Alec

May

One and a half years later

My cell rings, jerking me out of sleep. My heart jumps, that little voice in my head saying it's never a good thing to get a call in the middle of the night.

Fumbling, I grab my phone off the small table by my bed and freeze, staring at the name lighting up on the screen. When it goes off again, I almost drop the stupid thing, but then my hand tightens, determined I can handle this. So what if he's calling for the first time in almost two years?

"Yeah." My voice is raspy from sleep, and I fight to make sure I sound like I don't give a shit. At least I shouldn't. Not after all this time.

Silence meets me.

Worry makes my throat tighten. Why he's calling? Did

something happen? There's not really another excuse for him to try and get a hold of me anymore.

"Brand—Brandon. What is it? Is it Charlie?" What the hell would I do if something happened to my best friend?

"Shit," Brandon mumbles, the word making me want to break something. It means he didn't plan to talk. He would have hung up, but now he knows I'm worried about Charlie. "Charlotte's fine. Nothing's wrong with her. I needed…Never mind. I'm being fucking stupid. I have to go. She's fine."

And then the line goes dead.

"Shit!" My hand squeezes my cell. I'm doing everything I can not to throw it across the room. Pushing up, I sit with my legs hanging over the bed. I drop my cell so I don't break it.

Or call Brandon back.

I slam the door on the thought of calling Charlie. No matter what, Brandon wouldn't lie to me about her. If he said she's fine, she is. So what would I say? That Brandon called me in the middle of the night, and he's still such a part of me that I needed to talk? That after all this time with nothing from him—after how I won't talk to Charlie about him or how I didn't want to hear about him from her or Nate when they came back from New York last summer—that I'm all on edge after one call?

Fuck that.

I'm not doing this anymore. He's been the only person on my mind since the first time he came to Lakeland Village when I was fifteen. Five and a half years is enough.

I lie back down, wishing for sleep that won't come. Trying not to remember the sound of his voice. How it was almost broken, like his voice box hadn't been used in a while. And try to forget how he said nothing was wrong with Charlie but didn't say the same for himself.

What's the point? He's made it clear I'll never be worth the sacrifice. That I'll never be the one he'll let himself really want.

* * *

"Let me come over tonight?" Logan asks, as we stand in the parking lot of where I go to college—a whole half hour from Lakeland Village, where I've lived all my life.

On reflex, my eyes scan the area to make sure no one heard him. When I look at Logan again, he rolls his green eyes. "Even if someone heard me, Alec, they'd just think we're friends. I don't go to school here, so they don't know I'm gay, remember? Chill out."

"Funny, I thought we *were* only friends." He flinches, making me want the words back. He doesn't deserve me being an asshole.

Logan pushes his black hair out of his face. There's a little scar by his lip, I try not to pay attention to. He has both his ears pierced and a few tattoos. Logan has this skater look I never would have thought I'd be into but it works on him.

Grinning, Logan taps his shoe to mine. "*I* never said I only wanted to be friends with you. That was *your* rule. I'm biding my time. Sooner or later you'll come around. You liked what I did to you, Alec. You liked having my hands on you. I know you did."

Damn it. I did. Even hearing him talk about it, my body starts to react. Heat shoots through me, the urge to have him touch me again, hitting me full force.

Logan steps closer, lowering his voice, while I fight the urge to walk away. "You don't have to be ashamed." The sincerity in his words makes my palms itch with the urge to shove him. He's not being a prick, even though he has every right to be. Logan's way more understanding than I deserve. Here I've been pissed at

Brandon for walking away when I don't even have the balls for anyone to know who I am either. But for Brandon I would. Even if my own dad hated me, I'd do it for him.

Logan's voice is even lower when he adds, "We'll go as slow as you want. Let me show you how good it can be. Just don't kick me out this time, okay? We could be good together."

For a second, I let myself wonder if we could be. There's a part that knows he's right. He's patient as hell, I'll give him that. Not many guys would stick around after my shit. The first time we kissed, I kicked him out of my apartment afterward. I'd never kissed another guy except Brandon and even though on some levels it felt right, the masculinity of him, it was wrong too. He isn't Brand.

Things went slow after that, a few more kisses, but I always stopped him there. I was a fucking kid when I was with Brandon and we'd never really gone farther than making out. Even though everything inside me knows this is who I am, that doesn't mean it's easy. A little part of my brain still wonders if I can change it, or why I don't want to. Coming out would be like being cut open all the time, everyone seeing what's inside me. It's showing parts of me that people will judge me for and maybe even hate me for.

And yet Logan's still here. He's out but he gets that I'm not. I figured making him leave after the first kiss, and then the hand-job would be too much. What kind of guy loses his shit after getting jerked off?

Someone in denial about it and still hung up on someone else.

"I like you, Alec." He almost steps closer, but doesn't. "I also don't know how long I'll stick around."

A fear I don't expect spikes inside me. Logan's the only person in the world who knows I'm gay besides Charlie, Nate, and Brandon. It feels good to be...*me*, and with someone who likes who that is too.

Do it. Tell him to come home with you. Stop being scared. Stop wanting Brandon.

And that's the biggest part of this, isn't it? Brandon. All day I've thought about his call last night. I've almost called him twenty times, but found a way to stop myself. Why the hell can't I let him go? I need to be who I'm supposed to be. I look at Logan, at the muscles I like and his strong hands. Unlike Brandon, he wants me.

"What time?" My brain turns off, so I can't over think this.

"Yeah?" Logan replies.

"Yeah. I—"

My cell phone rings cutting him off.

"Hold up," I tell him, which makes him roll his eyes again. Charlie's name pops up on the screen. I can't get used to calling her Charlotte, which she goes by now. We grew up together, working and spending time at The Village, her family's lake resort here in Virginia. I've called her Charlie since I could talk.

"What's up?" I say into the phone, trying not to stress that it's somehow linked to Brandon's call.

"Alec…"

The hairs on the back of my neck rise at the way she drags out my name. Something's definitely wrong and it has to do with Brandon.

"What happened?" Leaning against my truck, I try to ignore my jackhammering heart.

"He's okay. I need to tell you that first. Brandon's okay."

"What happened?" A vice squeezes my chest.

"There was an accident. He was out 4x4-ing with some of his teammates. They hit a tree and Brandon's chest hit the steering wheel."

A sharp pain hits me between the ribs at that.

"I don't really understand all of it, Alec, but the impact tore one of the arteries that goes to his heart. He had to have heart surgery."

My fist tightens, my jaw clenches. "Heart surgery?" Holy shit. The world starts spinning. Logan's hand shoots out and grabs my shoulder. "What?" My voice cracks.

"I didn't know if I should call you or not. I know that's wrong. I didn't want you to hurt anymore, but I don't know what to do. He's having a hard time, Alec. As soon as he left the hospital, they were able to bring him home to New York, but he won't talk to anyone. Nate can hardly get anything out of him. Three of his teammates flew over from Ohio, but he doesn't want to see anyone."

He called me, pops into my head and I feel like a prick for thinking it. That shouldn't matter right now.

"I'm sure he's scared. Worried about losing football…"

And I know what he does when he's scared—he runs. Closes himself off.

Before he used to talk to me.

"He could have died," she whispers.

"I'm coming. Don't tell him, okay? But I'm coming." It doesn't matter that there's still a month left of school or that I don't really have the money. Nothing else matters.

She says something in the background and I hear Nate say "thank you." Without a word, I hang up the phone.

"Logan—"

He moves back. "It's him?"

The only reply I can give is a nod.

"I guess you better go then."

"I'm sorry. I'm really sorry." I don't have time for anything more than that. I fly my piece-of-shit truck back to my apartment and throw some of my stuff into a duffel. I check my bank account before I go, and then head to the airport. On the way, I call the moving company where I work, and tell them there's a family emergency and I won't be in for a few days.

Family? Yeah right. They have to know it's a lie, since all I have is Mom and Dad, but they don't call me on it.

Because of a delay, I don't get into New York until early the next morning. If I trusted my truck more, I would have just driven in.

As I'm waiting by the curb, a white BMW pulls up and Charlie steps out of the passenger seat. Her arms wrap around me, and I squeeze her tightly.

"You shouldn't have waited so long to tell me." I get the reasoning, but I'm still pissed.

"I didn't know. We wanted to see what would happen and then when he made it out of surgery...I didn't know the best thing to do. You never wanted to talk about him, and it's only been a little over a week since he got out of the hospital."

I would have hated myself if he'd died and I didn't even know he was hurt. "This is different, Charlie. You know I'd want to know this." Before I pull away, I kiss her forehead so she knows it's okay. Then I toss my duffel bag into the back and climb in.

"What's up?" I say to Nate who's in the driver seat. Things have never been real great between us. From the first time they summered in Lakeland Village I was jealous as hell of him. He was the first guy who Charlie ever paid attention to other than me. Even back then I knew I felt things toward guys, but no one knew. Charlie was my best friend. I loved her. Things would have been okay with her. I thought I could be happy with her one day and more importantly, I could make her happy too.

Nate changed that for her. The way Brandon changed things for me.

Even though Nate and I are technically cool now, I'm not sure we'll ever be close.

Still, he turns around before pulling away and tells me, "Thanks for coming…My parents are worried. I didn't know what else to do."

He's going to be pissed. If he wanted me here, I would have been here for the past year and a half. "No problem."

We're quiet most of the way to their house. A couple hours drive is a long time to be with my thoughts. I can't stop wondering if it was right to come, how it will be to see him and other shit I have no business thinking about. When we're close I need to make conversation so I ask, "How's Joshua?" He's their little brother. He was born premature the last summer we all spent together—the only one we spent here instead of Lakeland Village. I guess their parents had decided with both their kids going to college, they weren't ready to be alone yet. So with two boys in college, they also have a two-year-old running around.

"He's a monster. Healthy and growing like crazy, but a terror," Nate answers, before killing the engine in their driveway.

"What'd you tell your parents?" I ask. They're not even my parents and I know they'd still love Brandon if they knew. They don't talk about "faggots" the same way my own dad does, but I never gave Brandon hell for not being able to tell them. We each deal with being gay in our own way.

"They know you're his friend. They know you're Charlotte's best friend. We said you wanted to come see him."

I nod before getting out of the car. It doesn't seem like their parents are home when we get inside their quiet, oversized house. My stomach hurts like hell. It feels like something's burning its way through. I'm scared to see him. Scared he'll tell me to go. The first time he walked away stung enough. The last thing I want to do is go through it again.

"He looks pretty bad. I mean, he's okay, but he has the scar on his chest. He's already lost some weight because he's not eating the same or doing anything." Charlie's obviously nervous and rambling.

"It'll be okay." Really, I'm not sure it will be. *You can do this. Be strong. He's okay...*

I know exactly where his room is. I snuck into it a lot, in the middle of the night, that last summer. When we reach it, we all three stop a few feet from his door.

"Mom and Dad shouldn't be home for a while. If they get here, we'll make sure they don't bother you." Nate leans on the wall, looking a little nervous. I'm sure thinking of his brother with another guy weirds him out.

Nodding, I take a deep breath before going to Brandon's door, and knocking.

"Tired. Don't feel like talking," his voice croaks out. It sounds tired. It sounds broken.

Pushing it open, I say, "I don't care."

I actually see him tense but ignore it. Closing the door behind me, I click the lock and walk over to the bed. *Brandon.*

He does look smaller, but his dark brown hair is the same, kind of longish and messy. He still looks like the jock football player he is. I used to tease him about that. I've always played and loved ball too, but despite his hair color, Brandon always looked like the golden boy, the football player.

The lamp by his bed is on. He's got his dark blue blanket up to his waist and he's wearing a white button-up shirt. I see a bandage or something through it. *Because they cut his chest open to fix his heart.*

Turning his head to the left he looks at me, his face thinner, but his jaw still tight and strong. "What if I can't do it?" he whispers. "It's who I am."

Football. It always comes back to that. I also can't help but relax. Even after all this time, he talks to me. "No, it's not. It never fucking has been."

I drop my bag on the floor and kick out of my shoes. My whole body craves to touch him so I know he's really here.

It doesn't matter that Charlie and Nate are in the house, that his parents could come home, or that we haven't talked in a year and a half. That he might shove me away or that he cracked open my chest the same way the doctors did to him, only no one put mine back together again.

He's hurt. He could have died. I know him. He needs me.

I sit on the bed, turn, and lie down on my side next to him, my breath making the hairs on his arm move. *Don't push me away, don't push me away.* When he doesn't everything inside me lets go, all the time between us disappearing and it's that last summer again when we lay in this same bed the same way.

Neither of us talk, but Brandon leans down, rests his cheek on the top of my head...and exhales. "I had surgery on my heart..."

I wince. "I know."

"Eighty percent of the people who have torn artery on their heart die before they make it to the hospital. They bleed so fast..."

I didn't know that. But I don't tell him, knowing he just needs to talk.

"Did they tell you it was an artery that brings blood to the heart? I was bleeding inside. It was close...I could have..."

"You're here." *We're here.*

"I'm so fucking tired." His voice cracks. I want nothing more than to fix it.

"Go to sleep. I'll be here when you wake up." I can't stop myself from waiting for it—waiting for Brandon to say he can't. Or ask me to get up, or do what they said he did with everyone else and tell me he doesn't want to see me.

But he doesn't.

Brandon's... quiet, and I'm too afraid to even move. Soon, his breathing evens out and I know he did what I asked. A stupid part of me wishes I'm what he was waiting for since the injury happened. It feels good believing I can calm his storm.

And makes it even shittier that despite it all, he still walked away.

Chapter 2

Brandon

"Do you think what we do is wrong? Seriously, I mean. People say so much shit. It has to come from somewhere, right?" I sit next to Alec, in the woods. It's one of the few times we've been able to sneak away this summer. All through the rest of last year I swore I wouldn't do this when I saw him. Last summer, I was with Charlie's sister, Sadie. That made it easier. Hell, we were just friends anyway. Fucking sixteen and fifteen years old.

But I knew he made me feel different. I knew Alec looked at me differently too.

"I don't know," Alec finally answers. We're sitting so close, our legs touch. I want to reach over and grab his hand. If it was Sadie, I'd do it without thinking.

"And we're not really doing anything yet," Alec laughs. He's like that. He's good at being the center of attention and making people forget the bad shit.

"But we want to…" I whisper, surprised I do.

His head snaps toward me. His bright blue eyes, trying to see through me, I think.

"I mean, you said…when we talked. You do want to, right?" I hate that I sound like such a pussy. I'm older than him. I shouldn't sound like I need to hear his answer so much, but then, if he feels the same, it's not just me. If there's something wrong with us, at least we're wrong together.

"You know I do. And I changed my mind about my answer. No, there's nothing wrong with what we're doing."

I exhale a deep breath at his words. It's stupid. I know it's not really wrong. Gay people are getting married and things are changing, but seeing it and having it be me are two different things. Plus—I pick up my football—I can't have both. Things might be changing, but not on that field.

He's so fucking gay.

Stop being such a fag.

I couldn't share a locker room with a queer.

Comments. Words people say without thinking. None of them directed at me, but I still hear the words. Maybe more than anyone else.

"Even if other people don't get it, it's not wrong. Especially since they don't know." Alec pushes to his feet, holding out his hand for the football. "Let's play. One day when you're in the NFL, I'll be able to say I used to play ball with you."

Standing, I smile, somehow feeling lighter. He does that to me.

"You won't have to say it, because everyone will know… even if we don't, you know…we'll still be friends. Maybe you'll be playing with me and it'll be on ESPN—our story. Best friends who spent every summer together and then went to play in the NFL together."

The smile slips off Alec's lips and I wonder if I said something wrong. Without thinking, I reach up, and touch his face, then his hair, and let my hand slide down. Then I step closer, my hand at the nape of his neck. It fits perfectly there and he smiles again.

No matter what anyone thinks, it doesn't feel wrong. It feels better. He makes me better.

* * *

I knew he would come.

When I made the call, that wasn't my plan. Or maybe it had been, but I didn't admit it to myself. All I knew was I had so much shit going on in my head: the accident, the statistics, that I probably should be dead, that I had surgery on my heart…that I'm scared to fucking death I won't play ball again. The doctors say anything is possible. I'm already a miracle for living, but lying here, knowing my chest was open and that I have to heal and my body is weak, it doesn't feel like it.

For someone who only knows myself as a football player, even a 5 percent possibility of not being who I was, feels more like 95 percent. What if my endurance isn't the same? Or my muscles or my breathing? What if I can't take a fucking hit? Who am I if I'm not Brandon Chase, number forty-three?

I'm not like Nate. I didn't do well in school because I liked it. I found a way to do good so I could play ball.

All that stuff is overloading my brain and taking me over. I want a way to let it out, but it's all too raw. There's no one who knows all my insides, except the person I hurt, ran away from, and then called when I felt alone.

"I have to piss," is the first thing that comes out of my mouth when I wake up. It should have been "thank you."

Alec gets up, without making eye contact with me. "Can you...are you able?"

His question hits a nerve, making me feel even more raw. "I can go to the bathroom by myself. Can you...can you help me up though?"

He finally meets my eyes and it feels like I'm under the knife again. Only this time, I'm not unconscious. I feel every cut and stitch. I bleed.

Chill out. You're cracking up.

Alec reaches for me, and I let him. Wraps his arm around me. I let him do that too. He feels harder than he used to and I wonder if he's playing ball or just working out more.

When we get into the bathroom, I wait for him to leave.

"Are you...?"

I shake my head. We are definitely not going there. "Wait right outside. I'll tell you when I'm done."

My chest aches, this stabbing pain piercing through me. My legs are so weak, I have to sit down to pee. After I wash my hands, I say Alec's name. The door pushes open and he's right there.

"I had to piss like a woman," I say, not sure why I said it.

"So even more has changed than I knew about?" He grins. A small laugh falls out of my lips. Another pain hits me, and I grab on to the counter. Alec is right there, holding me again.

"Asshole."

"But you smiled."

Yeah...yeah I did. "I'm tired of lying down. I want to sit." Alec helps until I'm sitting on my bed, before he's down right beside me again. Our legs are touching and I can't help but remember that time, years ago when we sat like this together. One of the many times.

The urge to reach for him hits me again, but I definitely

can't now. *I don't want to, I don't want to, I don't want to.* "You shouldn't have come."

"I know. You had to know I would."

I look down at our legs leaning next to each other. "I also shouldn't have wanted you to. We both know I did though."

"I didn't."

You didn't? How can you not know?

That pain in my chest hits me again and I wonder if it's not because of my surgery—if it's not because some stupid fucking night out broke something in my heart. Possibly took away who I am. Maybe the pain will always be there because of losing Alec. My torn artery, or whatever the hell it is, is nothing compared to that.

"Alec…"

"Don't. We're not doing this right now. I came here because you were hurt, not so I can try and pull useless words out of you. We both know regardless of what either of us says or how we might or might not feel, it doesn't change anything."

He's right. And I know that's mostly my fault.

"But I'm glad you're here. I just want…"

"When we're alone, it's like nothing else matters, right? Fuck everyone else." I hold the back of Alec's neck, liking the way my hand fits there.

"Fuck 'em," he adds, touching my hair.

It's the only time I really feel like me. Where I'm most comfortable and can do or say whatever I want. I'm just me. No games. No fronts. Only Brandon.

"Do you need to take any of these, or anything?" Alec's words rip me from the memory.

"The pain meds."

"Why didn't you tell me you were hurting?" Alec looks through the bottles and grabs my Vicodin. He opens it and shakes one into my hand. "I'll get you some water."

After grabbing the cup from the table, he heads toward the door, and this stupid ridiculous fear surges through me. "That bathroom's good. You can get it from there." *Don't go.*

He turns, nods, and then goes to my bathroom, walking out a couple seconds later with the glass full of water. After I take the pill, he puts it back down.

"Thanks for coming, man." It feels like such a nothing, thing to say. It doesn't say the half of what I want it to.

Alec shakes his head like he gets it.

"I need to clean my incision. My parents should be home any time too. They said around seven and they'd bring dinner. If I don't do it now, my mom will try to do it for me. I know she wants to help, but she's driving me crazy. I wish I had my own place out here."

"You still in the dorms back at school?" Alec asks.

"No. I have a little apartment. You?"

"Me too. It's like thirty minutes from Lakeland Village. Want me to help you back to the bathroom?"

"I think I can do it." He flinches as though I hit him.

Slowly, I get to my feet. It's just as slow for me to get to the bathroom, Alec right next to me the whole time. "I have no appetite, so I'm losing weight and getting weak. My wound burns and itches all the time." I don't know why I say those things to him, because I haven't said them to anyone else.

"It won't last forever. You'll be kicking ass in no time."

I don't reply to that, because I'm not sure how. It takes my fingers a couple tries to get each button on my shirt undone. Alec stands next to me. Even though I'm not looking at him, I feel his eyes and I wonder if I should ask him to leave. But then, why should I? It's only my shirt.

I wish I knew why I was standing here with him. Why I let him in when I don't want to see anyone else or why I let him help me, when it pisses me off with other people. Why I whispered those fears about not playing that I keep locked away from even my brother. But then, it's always been like that when it's just us.

When I get the last button undone, I look at Alec, his eyes on my chest.

"No staples?" he asks, eying me.

"There's stuff inside holding me together." Really I don't feel together at all. Slightly weak, I lean against the wall.

"The tape?" Alec asks.

"Stays on." He nods and then turns on the water. Grabs one of the folded washcloths off the shelf.

"This soap?" He points to a bottle and I nod.

Alec sets down the washcloth and washes his hands before wetting the rag.

"What are you doing?" My voice is raspy.

I know what he's doing.

"It's not a big deal. Your brother would do it. Your mom would do it. I'm just helping."

But to me, it's a big deal. A big fucking deal even though I wish it wasn't. Or maybe I don't wish that. It's so hard to keep it all straight. I don't know how to be gay and play ball. I don't know how to be the player I've grown up thinking I am, if I'm into someone who's not a woman. But I don't wish Alec gone either. It's strange to even think of never having met him.

I flinch when the warm cloth touches my chest.

"Am I hurting you?"

"I'm not going to break," I bite out, frustrated. My mind has always been weak, but not my body.

The wall holds me up, while Alec washes my incision. It

Chapter 3

Alec

I leave Brandon's room before he wakes in the morning. It was weird staying in there last night. I know Nate probably thought he was doing Brandon a favor, but he wasn't.

I take my bag with me when I go.

Charlie's downstairs when I get there. She looks up at me from the couch, this strange, unreadable look in her eyes. I used to know everything about her. She knew almost everything about me too. Then Brand and Nate came and everything changed for both of us.

Her voice is hopeful when she says, "I told Nate I wanted to spend a few hours with you today. I thought maybe we could go into the city."

"Cool. I kind of need to get out of here."

Charlie nods, more sadness on her face.

I take a quick shower and then get dressed. Before going downstairs, I stall at Brandon's door for a second, wondering if I should go in and check on him, but I don't. It's too awkward and

I'm not in the mood for that right now. Charlie's waiting for me again, while Nate sits on the ground playing with Joshua.

There was a time Nate would have been pissed about us leaving alone together, but I guess knowing I've been pining after his brother since I was fifteen changes that.

We make small talk on the way to the train station, but I know something's coming. After we board and we're in our seats, she asks, "How'd it go last night? I mean…I know it has to be hard, because of everything."

I shrug. "It went as good as it could."

"He has three friends in from Ohio for the weekend and he's had us make excuses so he didn't have to see them. He hasn't eaten dinner downstairs once since he's been home, yet he let you in without complaint and he spent the evening with his family last night. You might not see it, but that means something, Alec. I'm sorry if it hurt you, but I want you to know, you helped give his family some peace of mind. You must have given some to Brandon too."

Dropping my head against the seat, I tell her, "Not enough to make it matter. Not to him."

She leans her head on my shoulder. "I don't understand it. I know he loves you. I *know* it. Why is it so hard for him?"

"You can't understand because you haven't experienced it. It's easy for people to say when they haven't lived it. And maybe it's easy for some people to do but…"

"You'd do it."

"How do you know that? I still haven't come out to anyone."

"But you would, wouldn't you? If you could be with Brandon?"

I shrug. "Yeah, I think I would, but that doesn't mean anything. It's simple to say, *I could do this, I could do that,* but a whole hell of a lot harder when you actually have to."

Charlie puts her arm through one of mine, hugging it, making me realize I missed having my best friend around. "I want you happy. Is there...I mean, have you? Is there anyone else?"

I laugh. She can hardly say it. I'm the same way, even with her. "I love you, Charlie, but I don't know if I can talk about this with you."

"You can talk about anything with me. We used to bathe together. I think that means we can share anything with each other."

I shake my head. "Not really. A fling maybe, but that's all."

"A guy?"

"Yeah."

"It's hard on Nate. He doesn't understand and Brandon doesn't say anything. If you hadn't told me when he called everything off, we never would have known."

The soft, probing tone in her voice, tells me exactly what she's doing. She wants me to tell her something, but no matter what, there's no way I can break Brandon's trust by telling them all his fears about coming out. How could I make her understand anyway? How would she get that he feels like football is all he's ever been good at. That it's what he thinks his dad is proud of him for. Not that his dad's all that into sports but because it gave Brandon something to excel at. That he's so scared of who he is that he made himself believe football is *all* he is, because it's easier that way.

"I can't, Charlie."

She sighs. "I knew you'd say that. You're the most loyal person I know, Alec."

There's nothing really to say to that, so I don't reply. For the rest of the ride into the city, we talk about other stuff. School, her and Nate's plans to go back to Lakeland Village this summer, like they always do. Her dad has MS. It was a tough time because he'd been working at their lake resort since he was a teenager. His wife left him and Charlie's older sister, Sadie, went with her and then Charlie wanted college instead of her family lake cabins. He's doing better though. He's in a wheelchair now, but he's also happier than he's ever been. He's engaged to a woman who really loves him. My parents also became partners with him and work there as well.

We don't stay in New York City too long and then we're on our way back to their house. The train ride back is even quieter than the one in. I'm sure the only reason we went in the first place is because Charlie wanted to try and talk to me about Brandon. It sucks that we don't know what to say to each other anymore.

Counting both train rides, we were only gone from the house a little over five hours.

Nate picks us up at the station. "Hey man…I thought you should know, Brandon's friends from school are here."

Automatically I tense up. Then I get pissed at myself because what's the big deal? I'm like Brandon and his friends. I play ball and talk shit and everything else. When Brandon and Nate used to come to Lakeland Village, he hung out with my friends and it didn't matter. We always had some kind of game going or were camping or fishing and it was never a big deal. All it is is hanging out.

But today we're seeing the people Brand's always been freaked out about. His teammates. The ones who don't know shit about him, but he pretends they do.

"I'm sure it's because they're leaving tomorrow and he feels bad that they came all this way." Nate catches my eye in the rearview mirror and I laugh.

"Holy shit, I must be acting funny if you're trying to make me feel better. You hate me."

"I don't hate you, man. Not anymore. I'm not going to say I didn't used to, but now…"

I turn away, hoping he'll shut up. What's he going to say? But now I'm the one who's into his brother? The one who's following him around like a goddamned puppy dog or something?

"It's not a big deal," I mumble. The conversation ends there.

When we get there, Brandon's mom is out in the garden. She tells us Joshua is asleep. I guess their dad is at work, which makes sense.

"Brandon's in the living room with his friends. It's so good to see," she tells Nate. "He's acting like he's back to his old self."

That's not him.

"I knew spending time with them would help. They're talking to him about football, and I can see how excited he is to heal so he can work toward getting on the field again."

Because he can lie about who he is there.

Then she looks at me, with eyes just like Brandon. "And you of course. It's so good for Brandon to have friends here for him."

"Thanks." I cross my arms. "I needed to get away for a couple days anyway."

"We're going to head in now, Mom." Nate tells her.

The three of us go back toward the house. The urge to stay out here is strong, but I push through it. We'll hang out and Brandon will play his game and then when they leave, it'll be normal again.

As soon as Nate opens the door, I hear one of them laughing at something. Brandon's house is huge, the sound almost echoing. We turn into the oversized living room, where everything is perfectly in its place. Brandon's sitting in a chair. Even from here, I can see how tense he is, but who the hell knows if it's because of them or me.

Two guys are sitting on the couch, one on each end, and another in a chair "'Sup?" Two of them say at the same time.

Nate and Charlie both tell them hi. I'm sure they've met the guys before. Charlie says they all fly out to games often.

"This is Alec," Brandon tells the guys. "He's Charlotte's best friend. We used to spend our summers in his hometown. Alec, this is Dev, Theo, and Donny. Dev's our quarterback. Theo's our kicker—"

"Best fucking kicker in college football."

Brandon and Donny laugh at Theo's interruption.

"You're so fucking gay. What you do wouldn't matter if my ass wasn't out there blocking for you." Donny, the beefy one, shoves him.

Brandon's eyes burn into me even though I'm not looking at him. Charlie freezes as Theo and Donny talk crap to each other and I pretend I don't want to slam my fist into all their faces. Maybe even Brandon's too. Not because his friends are assholes because everyone I know throws the word "gay" around like it's nothing but I can't even be his friend anymore? I'm Charlie's friend—oh and we used to vacation where he lives. What the hell is that?

Finally the guys stop and Donny stands and holds out his hand. "What's up, man? What did he say your name is again?"

"Alec."

Theo and Dev say hi too before Donny asks, "You play ball?"

I shrug. "Not really." It's a lie. I've always loved football. After meeting Brandon I used to secretly wonder if I could play somewhere one day too, but I don't so I know that "no" is the answer they're expecting.

"Alec was really good when we were in high school. He could have played in college if he wanted to." Charlie smiles at me like she just did me this huge-ass favor. I know she only wants to help, but she didn't. It's shitty, but they'll think it's a joke coming from her. If Brandon would have had my back, that'd be different, but he doesn't say anything.

None of the guys really say anything to that. I don't mean for it to happen, but my eyes find Brandon who's looking at the floor.

"She's kidding," I say and they laugh like it's a hilarious fucking joke.

"We gotta bail in a little while. Wanna go downstairs and hang out?" Dev asks Brandon.

"Sure," he replies. Brandon winces as he stands, and I wonder if anyone besides me notices. I wish like hell I didn't.

"You should be taking those stairs a hundred times a day. You've lost like fifteen pounds," Donny teases. "Get your ass in shape so you can get back on the field next year. We need our boy."

"Fuck, I got this. Nothing's holding me back. Come practice I'll be kicking everyone's ass in drills like I always have. No other running backs will be able to touch me." Brandon laughs and his friends do the same. He's hunched over a little as they walk to the stairs that lead down to their family room where they have the big screen TV and pool table.

I stand there waiting to see if he'll tell me to come. He knows I know how to fake it too. There's no reason not to tell us all to go down there with them, but he doesn't. It's not till they get to the door, that he looks over his shoulder right at me.

I make myself turn away.

* * *

Brandon and I manage to avoid each other the rest of the night. I chill with Charlie and Nate. When his friends leave, his mom doses him up with pain meds and he passes out.

I go to bed early, in the spare room, but don't sleep. To pass the time I play some games on my phone, before something makes me pull up Logan's number.

Hey. I text him.

Hey. How's your friend?

How are you? Brandon is the last person I want to talk about right now.

I'm cool…been thinking. Might be jumping the gun since you're there with your boy, but not sure I wanna keep doing this.

A deep breath leaves my lungs, and it feels like I don't have any air left.

He's not my boy, but I get it. You're smart to say that.

And he's a prick to fuck around with you.

The way I did you? I ask.

Nah. You never made promises. I just kept pushin'. You're hot. Hard not to.

A smile tries to pull at my lips. **I wish I didn't make it so hard.**

There's a pause before Logan replies. **You ever find your way away from your boy, you get a hold of me.**

Anger slams into me out of nowhere. I'm fucking pissed at myself and pissed at Brandon and even Charlie for calling me and telling me Brandon needed me when he doesn't.

K.

I toss my phone to the floor. Thinking maybe Brandon had it right all along. Maybe I just need to lie and pretend like he does. Get a girl and find a way to be happy.

I don't know how much later it is that I hear the door open, see the shadow slowly step inside before it closes again. My heart kicks up. My brain telling me to say, "Fuck off" but nothing comes out.

Brandon stands by the edge of the bed. It's dark as hell in here, but I know he's looking at me and I'm looking at him too.

"I'm sorry. I'm so fucking sorry," he says, his voice cracking. "I was such a pussy. I could have let you come down. It wouldn't have mattered. Christ, I'm so fucking sorry."

"You should be…and I'm sorry too. Come here." The words come out more easily than they should

"Ouch," Brandon whispers as he gets into the bed.

"Be careful." Reaching for him, I try to figure out how to help him or where to touch him.

"No. Just wanna hurry." And then he's lying down with me, but he's propped a little higher on the pillow. "I want to be strong. Why the fuck can't I be stronger?"

But it's not just him. It's me too. Having him or not, I could have come out. "Maybe we're not supposed to be. Maybe this is the way it's supposed to be for us."

I feel him shake his head. We're quiet for a little while when he asks, "Did I ever tell you about when I started playing ball?"

"No," I say, even though he has.

"I was fucking up in school. I was young, like second grade or something. The teachers kept saying I didn't try and that I interrupted in class. I got in trouble for a little while, but then Dad pushed and got me tested and they found out I was dyslexic. I didn't know what it was, but it made me feel stupid.

"They got me a tutor and it was this guy who loved football. If I worked really hard during all our sessions, we'd play football for fifteen minutes after every day. Found out real quick I was better at football than school."

"Shut up. You're smart. You worked your ass off and you do well now."

"Not as well as I play ball and I only did well so I could play.

I'm … I'm so fucking scared I'm going to lose it and if I do, I'll lose me. Even if it's not because of this heart thing, but because …"

"… of me." If he ever tried to be with me, that is. He thinks if people knew about us, he'd lose the team. I try to pull away, but Brandon's hand grabs my waist, his fingers digging into my skin.

"Not because of you. Because of *me*."

We've done this so many times in the past, even when we were a thousand miles away and only on the phone. That's how we really started—just talking. We could always talk.

"That's why I can't and I know that's fucked up."

I don't reply because there's nothing to say that will make a difference.

"Wanna know something else? I'm scared to start trying to work out again too. Scared I'll fail and lose myself and scared I'll succeed and have no choice, but to keep on being who everyone expects me to be."

That last part, I didn't anticipate.

Suddenly, I really want to touch him, but I don't know where or how because he's hurt. One of my hands finds its way to his chest, as I roll over and face him. Even though he's lost weight, I feel the muscles under the skin and the rough edges of his bandage.

If I wasn't so scared too, I'd do more. Be like Logan and let my hands slide under his shorts. He should be the first guy who I touch like that. It took us summers to work up to touching on the outside of our clothes when we were kids.

"I lied to you about Logan. I mean, he's real, but there's not a whole lot going on with us. He tried, but I freaked out. It's not fair that I push you when I'm just as locked in the closet as you are."

Brand tenses for a second. "I still hate that another guy has touched you."

"I hate that girls have touched you. Hate that you've probably fucked them and held them and gone out together with all your friends."

His silence is all the confirmation I need. When I start to pull away again, his grip tightens. "Once...I slept with someone once and I felt like the biggest piece of shit in the world. Even worse than with Sadie. I haven't even dated another girl since then. It's been a year, Alec. A year and the guys talk shit, but I can't do it."

It's the same as always, not that I'm surprised.

"I'm going home tomorrow." I need to get that out there now. All these things he tells me will make me hold on to him. I gotta stop holding on.

"You could stay." His words are so soft, I hardly hear him. "I want you to stay. The guys are gone. My parents won't think anything—"

"No. It's not that easy anymore." Even though the words hurt, I almost feel like they build me up too. It's time to step off the roller-coaster ride for good. Not to try and be straight either—to try and be happy.

Silence.

Finally, what feels like forever later, he asks, "Can I stay in here tonight?"

I nod and he looks down and I look up and I have to taste him. I lean forward, my lips on his, but I can't go slow. My tongue pushes inside and Brand moans. It's like our tongues are fighting, both trying to take possession of each other and his hand tightens on the back of my neck like it always does and if I just go lower...I can dip my hand under his shorts and wrap my fist around him and touch him like I've always wanted to.

I shift, hungry, urgent, crazy, wild, and try to push forward and—

"Ouch. Fuck!" he hisses.

"Shit. Your chest. I'm sorry. Are you okay?"

"I'm okay." His hand is still on the back of my neck. "Jesus, I fucking missed you."

We both relax back into the bed and just lie there. He pulls my hair and rubs my neck and again I wonder how this can be wrong. How feeling comfortable with him, how belonging with another person can cause so much pain and anger.

Finally, after hours of lying here, I'm almost asleep. Before I go out, Brand says, "When they fixed my heart, I wish they would have fixed me. Made it so I wasn't so weak."

I don't answer. Nothing will change it anyway.

When I wake up in the morning, he's not in my room.

Chapter 4

Brandon

I sit in our workout room, earbuds in with no music playing like I've done way too many times over the past month since Alec left. That tingle beneath my skin whips through me, hungry, eager for the sting in my muscles and sweat beading on my skin that I used to get lifting. That I should feel take me over right now as I pretend to work out again.

I want it. Want that burn and pain because it's been a part of my life for as long as I can remember. Every time I try, I see my muscles failing. If I don't try, I won't discover I can't do it. Yeah, I know I'm not doing it now but that's by choice, not because it was taken away from me.

Even to myself it doesn't make sense but it doesn't stop me from using the excuse. A lot of things I've done haven't made sense.

Before Alec has the chance to climb out of that dark corner I make him hide in in the back of my head, I push to my feet. My T-shirt hangs on me looser than it used to, but taking it off is worse because then it's easier for the scar to taunt me.

For the millionth time I wonder if I shouldn't have refused the rehab and personal trainer my parents and my team tried to force on me. At least then I wouldn't have a choice about doing what needs to be done. All the doctors are enough though. I know what I'm doing. I don't need someone breathing down my neck.

Turning, I head for the staircase from downstairs to the main level of the house. It's only about ten steps, which I take two at a time. As soon as I round the corner, I see Nate sitting in a chair. "Done pretending to lift already?"

My brother didn't used to call me out on my shit as much as he does now. I'm caught between having respect for him and being pissed off. "Can still kick your ass, little man." I fall into a chair beside him.

Laughing, he shakes his head. "Asshole."

Well we know that's the truth. I'm pretty sure Alec would say the same thing. Without asking, I grab his water bottle from in front of him and take a drink. "Where's Charlotte?"

"She's got some volunteer thing going on at school. It's her last day and then we gotta get ready to go to Virginia."

He takes the bottle from me and finishes it off and all I can do is sit back and watch him, wondering if he knows how fucking easy his life is. I'm not mad at him for it. More power to him, but it must be nice not to have people who expect certain things out of him. He has the girl who he's been in love with since he was fifteen years old. He's smart and has plans that he really wants. His life is perfect.

"Cool." I screw around with my iPod, not wanting to look at him. If he starts talking about Lakeland Village I run the risk of him talking about Alec.

"So you scared or what? Why do you sit down there and pretend to exercise every day?" He gets this cocky smile on his face and I know he realizes exactly what he's doing.

"I'm not scared. That's ridiculous. Maybe I'm just not feelin' it anymore."

"Sure you're not." Nate pushes to his feet, and my arm automatically flies out to grab his arm.

"What the hell is that supposed to mean?"

He grins again. "That you're full of shit."

Shaking my head, I let go of him. "You're a comedian now?"

"You make for easy jokes. Did you hear the one about the football player who didn't love anything like he loved ball, but when he ran the risk of losing it, he sat back and pretended to fight for it, while he really did jack shit?"

Anger burns through me. Without realizing I even got up, I have Nate's shirt in my hands, and I've pushed him against the wall. "Fuck you."

Nate's breathing heavy when he says, "I'm sorry. Shit. That was an asshole thing to say."

My fingers don't work when I try to pry my hands away from him. I've never hit my brother in my life but my fists are begging me to do it right now. "You don't know what you're talking about."

"How am I supposed to when you don't *tell* me anything? I thought...I thought we got over that when you told me about Alec. I'm your brother, man."

At that my hands slip away and I turn my back to him, not because I'm pissed at him, but because I'm an asshole. Growing up we were like any brothers, I guess. We fought all the time but we still always had each other's backs. He didn't know that practically everything he knew about me was a lie. Yeah, I was all about ball but not for the reasons he thought.

Then...then I told him about Alec and I know he thought

that meant things would change but I'm still lying. The only person who really knows who I am, I push even farther away than I do everyone else.

"Talk to me." Nate steps around me.

"You're hanging out with Charlotte too much. You're getting soft, bro." He rolls his eyes at my attempt at a joke. "It's not that big a deal. I'll figure it out like I always do, yeah? Maybe it just feels good to have a little break from the routine. There doesn't always have to be some huge reason behind everything, Nate."

Before he has the chance to reply, my cell rings. As soon as I pull it out of my pocket, I shake my head. "Hey, Mom."

"Hi, sweetie. I wanted to check in with you to see if you need anything before I come home. It'll be about an hour or so."

Nope. And if I did, I could get it myself. "I'm good. Thanks though."

"How's your day? I bet it feels good for you to be back in the gym."

Tightening my fist, I squeeze my phone. She's trying to help and that makes me feel even worse about my anger, but it's hard. Our parents have never really been the clingy type. Dad was always working at the university and Mom always had her own projects going on. Even when we'd go to Lakeland Village for the summer, we did our own thing. Nate and I have always been used to having freedom and pretty much doing what we want. Every time she asks me if I'm okay it reminds me how much shit has changed. I mean, I don't want to make it sound like they were shitty parents. We knew they loved us, they just weren't overly involved.

"I've always loved working out." It's not a real answer but she doesn't seem to notice. Mom rambles on for a few more minutes before I manage to escape the conversation. Tossing my cell to the table, I look at my brother. "I know they just want to help but they're driving me crazy."

"Better you than me." Nate crosses his arms.

"Whatever, asshole." He stumbles a little with my soft push. "I'm thinking about heading back to Ohio, spending the summer there. A few of the guys are local so I can get back into routine with them. Or maybe heading to NYC or something. I'm going to lose it if I have to stay here." I've never spent a summer in Ohio. Never spent the summer in NYC either. It's always been home, vacation with the family, or Lakeland Village.

"You don't want to spend the summer in Ohio. You don't tell me shit but even I know that. Mom and Dad will flip."

"I'm twenty-one years old. It doesn't matter if they like it." He's right about the rest of it. I don't want to be in Ohio. I don't want to be here either. Like always, I don't know where in the hell I want to be.

Jerking my phone off the table, I try to ignore the tightening of my muscles and the tick in my jaw, as I head out of the room. I get to the stairs when Nate's voice stops me. "Go to Virginia."

One foot is on the bottom stair, one hand on the railing but I don't turn back to look at him.

"What else are you going to do, man? Mom and Dad won't get off your back if you're here. You don't need to be in Ohio right now and you know it. It'll be like when we were kids. Charlotte and I will be there and…"

Slowly, I turn around. I'm not sure what makes me say it—if I'm trying to be a prick or if I really want to know but the words come out regardless. "Is it hard for you to say his name because it's Alec and you've never really liked him or because you hate the fact that your brother's into a guy?"

Nate's always been laid-back. He relies on facts, he's honest about how he feels and he's fair. He looks like I punched him in the face. The set of his jaw and the ball of his fists tell me he wants to hit me.

"Fuck you, Brandon. You're turning into an asshole. I'll admit something to you. I'm glad you're not with Alec but it's not because he's a guy, it's because you don't deserve him. Not anymore."

He shoves his way past me; for the first time, someone in this house is not careful with me after the accident. There's an ache in my stomach because of the reason, and because of what I said but it feels so fucking good to be treated normally too.

It doesn't change that Nate is right.

* * *

Twirling my football in my hand, I lie in bed, thinking about what Nate said. I watch the brown leather spin, over and over. It's a nice ball. It used to be Alec's favorite until he gave it to me. No matter how many times I told him no, he kept telling me to take it. The truth was, I had another one just like it back home. I knew he didn't.

Yeah, he could have gotten another one but things weren't as easy for him as they were for me. And he'd won a big comeback game with it in high school. People who aren't into sports don't get shit like that but that ball meant something because of that win. It was lucky.

But he wanted me to have it and as weak as it makes me sound, I wanted it too because it was his. Every summer after that I brought it with us to Lakeland Village. It became my lucky ball even though I never played with it at home or school.

When I look at it, I remember who I was when we met—who

I am with him. I mean, it's only a seventy-dollar football but it was his and it meant something to him but it meant more to Alec for me to have it.

He thought I deserved it. When I think about how big a prick I was after he came all the way here for *me*. The way I turned my back on him when Dev, Theo, and Donny were here and how I didn't stick up for him when they asked if he played or even how I just treated Nate. He tries to be the brother I'll never let him be, and I throw bullshit at him like I did earlier.

The guy I am now doesn't deserve something that was so important to Alec. He was right to walk away, doing it for a whole hell of a lot better reasons than when I left him.

But I want to deserve it. Want something even though I'll never let myself have all of him. I can still try to be the person who would be worthy of him. The kind of guy who could at least be man enough to be friends with him. To earn him.

Palming the football, I jump out of bed. Ripping my door open, I go out and head straight for Nate's room. Right after I knock, he opens it. Charlie lies on their bed. My eyes dart from her to him. "I'm going."

Chapter 5

Alec

"What are you doing when you get off work?"

I change the phone from one ear to the other as I sit in the passenger seat of the work truck.

Water or something is running in the background making it hard for me to hear Logan. He called not long after I got back from New York and I told him how things went with Brand. We decided to be just friends for real this time, which I'm thankful for. It's been cool having him around.

"Nothing that I know of. What the hell is that noise?"

He laughs. "I just got out of the shower. I'm shaving." This little flash of Logan standing in the bathroom with a towel wrapped around his waist flashes in my head. I smile at the thought. Before I wouldn't have thought about anyone except Brandon that way but in the month that I've been back, I think I'm really starting to get over him.

I have to. The trip to New York proved nothing will change with him.

It's too bad I couldn't have done it before Logan and I decided to only be friends, but maybe it's better that way. I don't have any friends who are gay and if we tried something and I screwed it up, it would be shitty not to have anyone.

"Are you imagining me naked in the shower?" Logan's question rips me out of my thoughts. My eyes flash to my work partner who's driving, wondering if he heard.

"No." And then because I'm tired of keeping my mouth shut all the time, I add, "In a towel." Sitting next to me, Rich doesn't even flinch. He doesn't know who I'm talking to but still.

"Ugh. Don't say shit like that to me. It makes it harder for me to keep up this friends thing. It wasn't that long ago I wanted to go there. You're the one who didn't, remember?"

Dropping my head back in the seat, I close my eyes. "I'm sorry. I'm—"

"Don't be sorry. You're a pretty good flirt and most of the time, I probably wouldn't even care if you practiced on me. Just not yet. You can't tell me you're over the asshole yet."

"He's not an asshole," automatically comes out of my mouth. Rich glances at me before his eyes find the road again.

"You proved my point, Alec. Now do you want to hang out tonight or what?"

"Yeah…sure. But we're not playing cards."

"We are *so* playing."

I don't know what Logan likes so much about cards. Maybe it's because he always kicks my ass when we play. "We're almost back to the shop. I gotta go."

"Grab pizza. I'll bring beer." Logan hangs up before I can reply.

"Uh-oh. Boss is waiting outside." Rich nods toward the building as we pull in.

"So?" He's been working here for a couple years. It's been less than one for me. It helps pay my rent while I'm in school and that's all I care about.

"Their son must be in town for the summer. That never goes well for the rest of us."

Before I can ask him what the hell that means, Rich gets out. I follow behind him when my boss calls, "Alec! Come here for a second."

A weight drops into my stomach and I suddenly get what Rich was saying. It's not that I really care about this job, but it helps pay the bills. My dad's already giving me shit about not helping out at the lake cabins this summer, but hell, I'm over it. I always expected the lake cabins to be part of my life—mine and Charlie's but that life would have been a lie. Being there reminds me of that. And being around my dad I think about why I wanted that lie.

When I get a couple feet from my boss, I stop. "Hey. Is everything okay?"

He crosses his arms, pasting this stern look on his face. "I hate to tell ya this, kid, but we're going to have to cut your hours. We'd like to keep you on call if that works for you. If not, I understand."

"Did I do something wrong?"

"No, no. If you remember, you were hired on as temporary." He rubs a hand over his bald head.

"Almost a year ago." But then, I guess that's why they do it that way.

"Alec…"

"I'll take my last check." I don't need to hear his words. It's not like working for them is what I wanted to do with my life. It's a shit job and I'll find another shit job or go back to working at the cabins.

Without another word, he turns to go inside. It's not a minute later he comes back out with a packet and hands it to me. I take it and walk away.

There's a pizza place not far from the shop, so I stop by and order one. It doesn't take them long to bring it out to me and when they do, I'm on my way to my apartment.

Logan's waiting outside my door when I get there with a brown paper bag. His black hair hanging in his eyes a little like it always does. "What's up?"

"Eh. Not much." I stick the key in the knob and unlock the door. "Lost my job. You know, another day."

He grins. "Guess it's a good thing I brought the beer." For a second I think about everything that's gone down with us in the past few months. I'm lucky he's still my friend. It's that thought that makes me feel like a dick because the first thing to pop into my head is how different it would have been if I'd told Brandon I got fired.

Pushing the door open, I nod my head for Logan to go inside. He does, setting the bag on my small kitchen table.

"I need to grab a quick shower."

"Don't get pissed if I drink all the beer and eat the pizza while you're gone."

I laugh as my stomach growls. "Yeah, since I can't trust you, I'll eat first." I click on the TV, the sound of *SportsCenter* filling the room.

He pulls out a twelve pack of beer, leaving two bottles on the counter before putting the rest in the fridge. After putting the pizza on the table, I open the box and grab some paper plates out of the kitchen. A minute later, I'm sitting on the couch in my living room, three pieces of pizza on my plate and a beer in my hand.

"I'm contributing to the delinquency of a minor," Logan falls down next to me, laughing.

"Screw you. I'll be twenty-one in a few months."

We're pretty much quiet while we eat because it's pizza and beer with sports on the TV. Once the food and my drink are gone, I say, "I'm hitting the shower."

"Want company?"

I freeze, halfway between standing and sitting before making myself push fully to my feet.

"I'm kidding. Friends, remember? I know how to be friends."

For some reason, I can't make myself move. It's not because I'm thinking about him in the shower with me. Okay, maybe that's a lie. Something like that's impossible not to think about when someone I'm attracted to says it but...

"I'm kidding, Alec." Logan stands. "Seriously. I'm giving you shit more than anything. Or maybe I'm a little horny too, but I don't want you to think I'm sitting here pining for you, okay? I would have said that to any guy I wanted. Damn you're conceited, aren't you?"

I shove him, and he falls to the couch. "Screw off. I wasn't thinking that." Though I kind of was. And even though it's cool to have him as a friend, I'd rather him leave, if I thought he was really that into me. I have enough shit for now and I don't want him hurt.

After I grab some boxer-briefs, basketball shorts, and a T-shirt from my room, I head to the bathroom. My shower is quick. I'm tired from work today and feeling like relaxing tonight. The longer I think about, the more pissed I get about my job. It's another shitty thing to happen in a long line of shitty stuff in my life.

I'm glad Charlie's coming back tomorrow. I miss having her around—wish I could have made it out of here like she did, which is funny. I used to be the one who told her Virginia is where we belong.

Logan still sits on the couch when I get out. I grab another beer, heading back to the living room.

"You look like such a jock." Logan teases.

"What the hell are you talking about?" He doesn't really play sports, don't think he ever did but it's not like he looks all that different than me. His muscles are cut, and he's wearing a pair of cargo shorts and a T-shirt like I am. Yeah he's pierced and tattooed but that's not a big deal.

"You just do. I can't explain it. If we'd met a few years ago, we wouldn't have been friends."

I shake my head at him. "I would have been cool with you. I've always been cool with just about anyone."

Logan laughs and I'm not sure why but it makes me laugh too. I'm about to sit down next to him when there's a knock on my door. Still laughing, I reach over and grab the knob and pull.

My mouth snaps shut, body tense as I look at the three people standing there. I can't find words and neither do they. Logan is suddenly silent behind me.

"Alec, we tried to call you, but you didn't answer." Charlie steps forward and gives me a hug. "Surprise?" she whispers in my ear.

I can't stop myself from looking at him, from wondering how he's feeling. He looks better than he did when I was in New York, stronger, but he's still smaller and his eyes still lonely.

"We can go, if this isn't a good time," Nate says when Charlie lets go of me. I break eye contact with Brandon and focus on his brother.

"We ended up coming a day early and thought we'd stop by and say hi," Nate continues.

Managing to find my voice, I signal for them to come in. "Nah. It's cool." Charlie, then Nate, and...

"Hey." Brandon pushes his hands in his pocket, before his eyes land on the couch. His jaw sets.

Serves you right, man.

I'm suddenly aware of everything. Of Brandon's shorts and the black button up shirt he's wearing. That his dark brown hair is a little longer. The feel of my still wet hair from my shower. It pisses me off, so I turn from him. Without saying anything to Brandon, I wait until he comes inside before pushing the door closed.

"Guys, this is Logan." He stands up and reaches for Charlie's hand. "Logan, this is my best friend, Charlie."

"Nice to meet you," she tells him.

"Hi." After telling her hello, he looks at Nate.

"That's Nate." They shake hands and then his eyes land on Brandon and I know he realizes who he is. Just like Brand knows who Logan is.

"And this is Brandon."

Logan smiles at him because that's just how he is. He holds out his hand. "What's up?"

Brandon doesn't move, his hands still shoved deep into his pockets. His arms are smaller, the muscles not as defined as they used to be and I suddenly feel like hitting him because I still notice him that way.

Finally when I think Logan is about to drop his hand, Brandon reaches out and grabs it. "Hey, man. What's up?" Dropping Logan's hand, he turns to me. "I didn't mean to interrupt."

Not, *we* didn't mean to interrupt. *I*. I wonder if he even notices he said it. Turning away from him, I reply. "You guys want something to drink?"

"Actually, I need to go to the restroom. Can you show me where it is?" Charlie's already heading for my hallway. The apartment is small. Two tiny bedrooms and one small bathroom. She doesn't need me to show her anything, but I still go with her.

She pushes her way in, pulling me in behind her before closing the door and turning on the water. "I'm so sorry! I didn't expect you to have someone here."

"Because I'm gay, doesn't mean I'm okay with being in the bathroom with you. We're not that close."

My lame attempt at a joke doesn't bring a smile to her face. Instead she sort of cocks her head and looks at me.

"What?" I ask.

"That's the first time you said you're gay. Even when I caught you with Brandon or the times you were in New York, you've never been able to admit it."

There's no real answer I have for that, so I move onto something else instead. "This is the second time you've kept something important from me, Charlie. You should have told me he was coming."

"I know. It was last minute and...I wanted him to come so badly. I think he needs to be here, Alec and I need you guys to be okay. Somehow I need you to be okay. Brandon's practically family to me now, and you've *always* been. It kills me to see you both in so much pain."

It's hard to stay mad at her when she says stuff like that because I know she really feels it. That's Charlie. She has a big heart and she would do anything if she thought it would help someone she loves. "I think we're as cool as we're ever going to be. He'll go back to living a lie and I'm—hell, I'm trying to get past the one I've always lived. That's all there is to it."

She grabs my hand and squeezes. "Are you and that guy...?" Studying me, I can tell she's trying to read me.

"Friends."

"That's all I'm getting out of you, isn't it?"

I smile at her even though there's still a fist around my gut thinking about Brandon being here and Logan meeting him. There's this screwed up feeling of betrayal slamming around inside me, though I'm not sure which one of them I think I betrayed. "I don't do the gossip thing either. Now let's get the hell out of here. It's not like everyone in that living room doesn't know what we're doing."

When I hit the end of the hallway, Logan is coming out of my kitchen with bottles of beer in his hands. He hands one to Nate, then Brandon and I almost ask if he's supposed to be drinking but keep my mouth shut. Charlie shakes her head when he offers one to her, so he hands the third to me. Logan winks my way, but I can't really get a read on him. Can't tell if he thinks of this as one big joke or if he cares that Brandon is here.

My couch is small so they've pulled the chairs from the kitchen into the living room, Brandon on one, Nate the other and of course Charlie sits next to Nate.

"You guys hungry? There's leftover pizza," I say as Logan sits on the couch.

"We're good," Nate replies at the same time that Charlie says, "We ate before we got here."

We're all quiet. I'm the only one standing and I know I look like an idiot—that I'm being one—so I take a seat on the opposite side of the couch as Logan.

Still, no one speaks.

Logan jumps in to save the day again, when he stands up and heads for the TV. "Anyone want to play some PlayStation? Most of his games are sports but he's got a few good ones in there."

"Hell yeah!" Nate stands and walks over by Logan and I can tell it's fake. Even Charlie's trying to pretend she's interested.

But not Brandon. I feel his eyes and know they never shift from me.

Chapter 6

Brandon

Alec and I have spent more time apart than we have together. I mean, I know that we've never really completely been together because we both tried so hard for so long to think this was something that we'd get over, but physically we've always, *always* been states apart.

We've only ever had the summer for those first three years and then a few weeks together the last summer. And a month ago, just a weekend, but still, every time I saw him, even seeing him for the first time after a year and a half, it felt right. I always felt right, happy. And in some ways I know that's a screwed-up thing to think because it shouldn't take another person for anyone to feel good but that's how it's been.

Until now.

Suddenly, Alec feels a million miles ahead of me—apart from me in a way he's never been, even when all we had were phone calls for months on end.

Only part of it is because of the bastard playing games and

laughing with my brother and Charlie, who my fingers itch to punch in the face. Mostly it's just because Alec is somewhere I've never been. He's going places I won't let myself go. My gut aches because of it but I'm also proud of him. And I want to go there with him too.

It would be me moving around his fucking apartment like it's mine, or me who he sat with, his hair wet after a shower, because that's what people do when they're with someone.

My hand squeezes the hot, unfinished bottle of beer in my hand.

"You guys here for the whole summer?" Logan asks with his eyes on me. It's the first time since we all sat down over an hour ago that Alec looks at me too.

"I'm here until practice starts in August," I reply.

Alec shakes his head at that but I'm the only one who notices.

"My dad runs a small lake resort not far from here with Alec's parents. Nate and I help in the summers." This from Charlie.

"I know. Alec told me." Logan's still eyeing me and I know what he's doing. He wants me to know that he and Alec are close.

Fuck you, man. Message received.

Charlie gets off the floor where she was with Nate and Logan before sitting in the chair next to me. My brother's lucky to have her. She's loyal as hell.

"Brandon's staying in one of the cabins with us," she continues.

I don't know if it's smart or not but I can't stop myself from asking Alec, "You're not working out there this year, are you? I know you have that moving job."

He shrugs, his face going a little hard but I don't think it's about me. "Who knows. Lost my job today so I might have to."

"Shit. I'm sorry. I know you don't want to…" Everyone's eyes are on me but right now, fuck them. I make myself continue, "I know it's shitty being around your dad."

Alec sets his bottle on the coffee table, leaning forward to put his elbows on his knees, but he doesn't reply. Just studies me like he can't believe I just said that. Like it was some big deal and I wonder if maybe it was. "We need to talk." He pushes to his feet, going right out the door without another word or glance at anyone.

"Another game?" Nate asks Logan.

Silence is all I hear and maybe it makes me a prick for not waiting for Logan to reply since I don't know if something's going on with them or not. Still, I stand to follow Alec, wishing there's a whole lot of other places I would have gone with him.

"Let's do it." Logan tells my brother as I close the door behind me. I walk until I find Alec standing by his truck.

"What the fuck are you doing here, Brand?" His eyes narrow at me in a way I've only seen one other time—when I called everything off between us.

"I needed to see you." It's the only answer I can give. Honesty, because it's all bullshit if I can't even be real with him.

"Fuck you, Brandon. You don't get to do that. You don't get to not talk to me for over a year, and then treat me like shit when I go to you when you need me. It's been too long. It's not that easy anymore." He's pacing in front of me, the muscles in his arms and legs tight. "We can't keep doing this. *I* can't keep doing it. What? You want me now because you think Logan does?"

Anger ripples through me, making my body feel as tense as his looks. Reaching out, I grab his arm, try to look him in the eye but he avoids mine. "I've always wanted you. You know that."

Despite how low my voice is, I know he heard when his eyes dart to mine.

I can't help but concentrate on the feel of his skin under mine—rougher than the girls' I've touched. His muscles constrict under my hand. Damn, he feels so fucking good that I want to squeeze tighter as though that will engrave the feel of him into me forever. It's a rush to every one of my senses, making me feel alive.

Alec doesn't give me a chance, jerking his arm from me.

"I didn't come to screw things up with us even more." I can't help but look around to see we're still alone in the parking lot. "I just…I want us to be friends."

Look at me, look at me, look at me.

He doesn't.

"I want to find a way to be the person who deserved you. Or maybe I never really did. I know this sounds stupid. I had that ball. Remember the football you—"

"Of course I fucking remember."

"Yeah, yeah I guess you would. I got in a fight with my brother and then I held it and…" I struggle to form the words in my head and then it's me pacing the way Alec just was.

"And what?" he asks.

We both pause, standing about two feet apart. "I realized I'm not the same person you gave it to. That guy might not have been out but he didn't hurt you. He didn't run the way I do now. I want to be him again."

When Alec is still silent, I add, "I know you're with—"

"We're just friends. I told you that. He's been a good friend."

When I haven't been. I get it. I glance away.

"I don't know if I want to be your friend anymore."

His words are a knife to my stomach, slow and deadly, taking out anything it finds in its way. And I deserve it. "Yeah…yeah, okay." I almost step toward him but make myself stop. "But I can't go. I don't know if that's the right thing to do or the wrong thing. I need to do this. It'll kill me if that hurts you but…I always felt like I found myself in Lakeland Village, ya know? I mean, I always wondered, but I never knew until I met you. I'm even more lost then I was then, Alec. I've got this stupid heart thing and everyone on my back. I need to figure shit out and, hell, maybe I'm being an asshole but I'm not ready to give up. Even though I can't have you all the way, I…"

Alec sighs. "You could've had all of me."

* * *

It's been two days since we left Alec's apartment. Charlie and Nate have been working around the cabins both days. It's strange seeing her dad in a wheelchair, but he's still out there helping any way he can. When we were kids and came here you could tell how much he loved it. The place was his life and it's obvious it still is, even though things are hard for him. He washes boats, and he shows people to their cabins and just like he always was, he's outside doing something.

I've always given my all to football like that. It's been my life. But when I look at him, I don't know if I want it to be my life forever. Hell, I'm not even fighting for it the way he's fighting to keep running the place he loves.

"Still can't believe you're the same kid who used to run around here, dragging Alec around and playing ball with him." Alec's dad steps up next to the porch where I'm sitting, taking my attention from Charlie's. It's the same cabin we used to rent when we came here with our parents when we were younger.

"I am, sir. I didn't drag him around though." I shrug. "He's good. I liked playing ball with him." Turning, I hope like hell

Alec's dad walks away. The last thing I want is to listen to him. He's always made Alec feel like shit.

"Good for *here*. He's not looking to get drafted into the NFL."

"Could if he wanted. I'm not sure if I'll be playing this year either."

"Alec doesn't fight the way you do. He's my kid and I love him but hell, even when it came to Charlie, he just let her go. He'd been in love with the girl his whole life. No offense to your brother." He laughs and the thing is, I know he doesn't realize he's being an asshole. It doesn't change the fact that I'd give anything to knock him out. To tell him Alec was never in love with Charlie and that he doesn't know shit about his son.

I open my mouth to say something, I don't even know what— to tell him to fuck off or that Alec fights harder than I ever do, but Alec's mom steps out of the office across the driveway and yells, "Honey! Can you come here for a second?"

"Be right there." He replies before looking at me again. "Good having you around. I'd love to sit down with ya sometime and talk football."

I can't help but wonder if he'd still want to talk to me if he knew I was in love with his son.

Chapter 7

Alec

"Not that I wouldn't love going to a barbecue with your family, where I'd have to pretend to be someone I'm not. I would do it if I wasn't going out with a guy tonight." Logan grabs his backpack out of the hall closet and smiles. "We're going hiking. Did you know I'm a kick-ass hiker?"

"No." I lean against the wall.

"Is your man still here? I thought we were going to have to throw down when he was here the other night."

"Is it shitty for me to admit I liked seeing him jealous?" I ask.

Logan laughs. "No. Not after everything he's put you through."

"It's not just him." On reflex I grab Logan's arm. "I know it seems like it but it's not. For the first few years I was just as determined to keep it under wraps as he was."

Pulling away, he shakes his head. "But you're not now. That matters, man." He sets his pack on the couch. Logically, I know he's right. It's Brandon who won't go there, and it's Brandon who keeps running, but I've never pushed him either. I never told him what I want.

"I know it's easy to make him the asshole but...he was always there for me too. Even when shit went down, he would have come to me like I did him if I was the one who got hurt."

There's not an ounce of me who doubts that. And he's still here now. It's only been a week, but I didn't expect him to stay.

Logan rolls his eyes. "No offense but I don't want to talk about him. Hiking was a much better conversation than this. Or even the fact that I bet I'll get laid tonight."

I can't help but laugh. And be jealous too. It shouldn't be this big a deal to be who I am, but it sucks when I don't want to do that without Brandon. "I really don't want to go out to the cabins tonight."

Logan starts putting the supplies he had on his couch, in the pack. "Nervous to see your guy?"

My groan is hard to bite back. "He's not mine. You should stop calling him that."

"You're his though." He stops to look at me. "Don't get me wrong, I hate the guy on principle but meeting him? It makes it harder to hate him when I see the way he looks at you."

Heat shoots through me. I know I should deny what he said, but I can't. I've never trusted anyone the way I trust Brandon and I know how he feels about me.

"It's not enough though." Logan sobers. "And you shouldn't have to wait. I mean, he's fucking hot and all but I'm better." His eyes hold mine for a minute and I try to figure out what he's telling me. If he's saying what I think he is.

Before I can reply, Logan continues, "Anyway, you should go. Zane will be here in a little while and I've got shit to do."

Pushing off the wall, I hold my fist out for Logan. He bumps it with his. "Have fun, man."

"Like there's any doubt?"

I'm pretty sure he's right. Shaking my head, I smile at him before walking out the door.

* * *

"Hello?"

The second he answers the phone, I start rambling. "I almost told him...Brand. He was talking about ball and this girl whose always hanging around that likes me and I was going so fucking crazy that I almost told him. I'm so tired of it. I just want..."

"Chase! Get the fuck over here, man. We're leaving with or without you."

Immediately I know he's with his friends from the team. Anger creates a whirlwind inside me that threatens to suck me under. "I'll let you go."

"Don't. Don't hang up." And then to the people he's with I hear him say, "Go ahead and go."

"What? You're ditching us, Chase. You're such a fucking bastard." They all laugh.

"You ever think something more important than you came up?"

I hear it in his voice, he's trying to play it off, maybe make them think he's going to meet some girl but I know—I know he's leaving them because he knows I need him. He always does.

There's sound in the background, which I think is Brandon walking away. There's a car door slamming and then he asks, "What did he say to you, baby? Jesus, I hate your dad."

That easily, things start to feel a little better. "Nothing... The same old thing, really. I'm just tired of hearing about when he was young, and what football meant and how many girls he had. He gives me shit about Charlie and hanging on to wait for her, and he doesn't even know..." That I'm in love with you.

"I'm sorry. I feel like such a prick. I should be going there this summer. Don't let him make you feel like shit. He doesn't know... He doesn't know how incredible you are."

"Yeah?" I ask him.

"Yeah..."

I practically hear him thinking on the other end of the line, hear him feeling like shit.

"Well obviously. Who could doubt that?" I tease and Brandon laughs. We talk for a few more minutes before I say I have to go. His brother will be here in two days and this is the first summer Brandon isn't coming. He's got some trip planned with some of the people on his team.

Two days later I'm outside working with Charlie when their car pulls up. His parents get out, and then Nate. I swear she almost lights up, this rush of jealousy setting root inside me. Not because I love her like everyone thinks but because I want what she has.

And then the other door opens, and Brandon gets out. Charlie runs up to Nate and jumps in his arms and now it's anger that takes hold of me—at Nate, at Charlie, even at Brandon. Because he came. He came when he knew I needed him but I can't show anyone how important that is to me.

* * *

The Village, what we call the cabins, is packed like it is every summer for the celebration. Charlie's dad started it years ago. It's a big welcome to beginning of the season where they have a cookout, music, and dancing on a small floor set up not far from the lake. When we were kids, Charlie and I used to have a blast here. When we got older, it wasn't as fun for her, but I still liked it. It was normal and at the time I wanted to hang on to every piece of normal I had in my life.

Now, I think that word's a lie.

My parents are more involved now, my dad running the grills as Charlie's dad travels along the new concrete path they put in to help him get around in his wheelchair.

Brandon is sitting in one of the chairs by the sand, picking at a football in his hands. My old ball.

"He's still having a hard time." Charlie steps up next to me.

"Not my business or my problem."

"Maybe, maybe not. It doesn't mean you don't care though."

I glance at her and she smiles. I can't make myself return it though. "Is he working out at all?"

"Nate says he's pretending to but not really doing it."

"Shit." It's hard to understand Brandon sometimes. He loves football, but he resents it too. He feels trapped by it but that love of the game is still woven into him. He's always been into fitness and even though he doesn't know where his head is right now, he has to miss the rush of a long run, of being active.

"I remember you guys always off doing something when we were teenagers. It used to drive me crazy. I didn't know how two people could be so into sports as you both were. I thought that's all you cared about. Now I'm wondering how much of that was really about the game and how much was you guys wanting to be alone together."

Without looking at her, I reply, "It started out about football. That was always part of it but then it was more about us."

Charlie sighs and I know she's sad for me. For both Brandon

and I. "We could both do something to change it but neither of us do." I watch as he runs his hand over the ball. "He said he wants to be worthy of it... That he wants to be the person I gave it to."

And he's not. I mean, I know he's still Brandon but he used to always joke around. He laughed, teased, and was happy. That's not what I see when I look at him anymore and it kills me.

"He's living a lie, Alec. You haven't come out, but you're still you. You have Logan and I have no doubt that one day, you'll be proud enough of who you are that you won't care what anyone else thinks. I don't know if he can do that."

"He can." The answer is automatic. "You don't know him like I do. He *can*." *He just won't.*

Brandon was the one who acted first on what we felt. He was the one who touched me first, and kissed me first and told me that he was falling for me. He'd been scared as hell but he'd done it. That piece of him seems to be lost now.

As if he knows we're talking about him, Brand looks up, his eyes landing right on me. His hair is messy. And even though he's not standing, I know his shorts are baggy enough that the top of his boxer-briefs sticks out, and that even though he's not in the same shape he was, his abs are so fucking nice.

He has the body of a running back—lithe, strong, and fast.

He nods his head at me, a half smirk tilting his lips. Right now, he looks like the Brandon I used to know. He holds up the ball and I know he's asking me if I want to play.

"You should go," Charlie whispers.

It's something so small but something we haven't done in so long. I miss it. Wish for that little piece of normal that used to be Brandon and me.

One step, then another. As I'm about to take the third, I hear, "Alec! Where are you going?"

I turn at the sound of Dad's voice as him and Mom walk up. "Nowhere. The party seems to be going well."

"It was a helluva hard day. It would have been nice if you could have helped."

Something brushes against my arm and I don't have to look to know Brandon came over to us.

"It's not his fault he had to work. You can't blame him for holding down a job." Mom wraps her arm through Dad's.

But I wasn't at work. I lost my job and don't plan on telling you.

"Doesn't mean it wouldn't help to have him around. This place is something we all took on. Charlie came home to help."

"I came to see my dad," Charlie says.

"Wanna come play ball?" Brandon asks.

I only glimpse at him before I turn away. He's trying to save me when he doesn't have to do it.

"Nah, that's okay. I need to take care of some stuff here. How are we on ice?" I direct the last part at Dad.

"I don't know. It's been a while since I checked. You need to refill the oil in the lamps. We need to talk about your schedule too, so I know how much you can help this summer."

"Do you always work long hours like the other day?" Brandon asks. This time I can't help staring at him. He knows damn well I didn't work late the other day just like he knows there's not even a job right now.

He sees I don't want to be here too… Without telling him, he sees it.

Brand looks at my dad. "We stopped by his place when we first drove into down. We had to wait forever since he worked late, but Charlie wouldn't let us leave."

She laughs. "I missed my friend. Plus, he was barbecuing for us. I didn't want to miss that." She lies just as smoothly as Brandon.

"Yeah it's tough in the summer. That's when a lot of people move." Which is true. I'm sure they're real busy.

"Are you going to be able to help much?" Mom looks at me.

"Probably not too much…I'll do what I can though." It makes me a jerk that I don't want to be here to help out my own family, especially when the money would come in handy. Being around every day isn't an option though. It makes me feel worse about myself.

"Damn it. I guess I'll have to figure something out. Way to leave us hanging." Dad laughs, playfully pushing at my shoulder. He's pissed though. He wouldn't argue for a second if I told him I'd quit my job and help this summer. He'd consider it being responsible for my family. It's what a real man would do.

Chapter 8

Brandon

Sitting in a chair on the porch of our cabin, I put my feet up on the wood railing. Nate and Charlie are inside and I really don't want to interrupt them. I feel like shit for busting in on their summer together. I'm sure they didn't want to share their cabin with Nate's screwed-up big brother but everything else had already been booked.

The air is still warm, sticking to me, even though it's late. Everyone left hours ago, and Alec before the rest. I couldn't read the look on his face when everything went down with this dad. I used to know that shit. Would know what's going on but it's obvious he doesn't want him to find out he's not working. I'm pretty sure it's because he doesn't want to spend the summer with him.

The flash of a light toward the driveway entrance catches my eye. Without seeing him clearly, I know it belongs to Alec.

It would be embarrassing as hell if anyone knew it but my heart rate kicks up the closer he gets to me. Alec doesn't stop when he gets to the porch, though. He just mumbles, "Come on," and nods his head toward the woods behind the cabin where we snuck off to so many times when we were younger.

Without hesitation, I stand and grab the flashlight on the railing of the porch. Taking the three porch stairs quickly I follow behind Alec as he weaves through the trees and to the spot we used to meet each other. When we get to the small clearing, he stops with his back to me. There's this ache in my gut, fears twisting up my insides, scared of what he might say.

Alec turns to face me. "Do you remember the third summer...?"

"When we got caught out here by Charlie?"

He smiles and some of the ache eases out of me.

"No, the beginning. How you weren't going to come but then I called you and you... showed up."

I take a step toward him. "Don't make a hero out of me because of that. I wanted to see you. I missed you."

"But you wouldn't have come. If I didn't call, you wouldn't have come."

Shaking my head, I say, "That's not a good thing. We both know I wanted to be here. The fact that I wouldn't have come makes me a pussy."

"The fact that I didn't have the balls to call you up and tell you I wanted you here, makes me the same thing."

When I don't reply, he continues. "I also remember you texted me that night. Nate was out with Charlie and we could have gotten caught sneaking out together but you still asked me to meet you. We took the football out and played in the dark. We kept tripping over shit and laughing. Remember when you fell and ran into that tree? That was funny as hell."

I shake my head. "That wasn't an accident."

"I know."

Quiet, he looks away from me. I shrug, even though he can't see me. "I could tell you were upset. Wanted to make you laugh."

We're silent for what seems like a year before he looks at me. "You don't laugh anymore."

No, no I don't. Not honestly, at least. "I feel like I'm being eaten alive, from the inside out and there's nothing I can do about it. Hell, it's my own fault. I pretend it's this stupid fucking heart injury that broke me but it wasn't. It was *me*." I've always been broken.

This time it's Alec who takes a step closer to me. Then another one and my breath catches.

"I want you to smile again too. It's in there, Brand. I saw it tonight. When you had the ball and then when we were talking to my dad."

I don't know if it's the right thing to do but it's the only thing I *can* do. Even if I wanted to, I couldn't stop myself. I step toward Alec and slide my free hand around the back of his neck. It only takes a gentle tug to bring him even closer, his hand moving to the same place on me that mine rests on him.

Alec closes his eyes and drops his forehead to mine. Neither of us talks, and I wonder if he's just feeling the way I am. It's that same rush that sweeps through me every time I touch him, my nerve endings like live wires, sparking with electricity. Everything inside me screams that this is right. He's right. How can anyone not understand this? How can I fight us?

"How do we end up like this so quickly?" he asks.

Quickly? It feels like it's been forever to me. In reply, I lean back enough so I can kiss his forehead. Kiss the corner of his lips.

I freeze against him when he mumbles, "I'm still pissed too…"

Everything inside me wants to keep going but the ache of knowing I hurt him is stronger. "Shit, I'm sorry. I thought. I don't know what I thought."

When I try to pull away, his hand fists in my hair, his grip tightening so I can't move away from him.

"I'm not saying no. We both know how this will end but I can't stand having you here and not being close to you either."

"I know." I run my hand through the back of his hair. Squeeze him because it feels so fucking good just to touch him again. "I'm sorry. Nothing I've ever had feels as right as you."

Alec pulls far enough away from me that we can look at each other. "Holy shit, you've gotten sappy."

I laugh, and it's a real laugh and I can tell he knows it because Alec's hold on me tightens and he's smiling too.

"Don't make me kick your ass."

Alec steps back. As he does I let my hand trace a path down his back. He's firm and muscular, making me wish like hell I could take his shirt off. Feel the contour of his body that matches mine.

"Can you borrow Nate's car tomorrow?"

I almost brought my truck to Virginia too but decided not to. "I'm sure I could."

"Drive down to my place. Hit the gym with me and then we can…I don't know, hang out or something after."

"There it is. I see your ulterior motive now. You're just trying to get me to train." There's a playfulness to my voice I haven't used in so long.

"Yeah, right. I know you. You don't do anything you don't want to do. Get your ass down there and let me show you up."

I give him a small nod because this feels like something for *me*. It's not training to get into shape for football. It's not trying to get past my injury. It's doing something I want to do, something I like. It feels like those days when we were younger and we played ball or whatever the hell we wanted and had fun.

He tells me a time and then says he has to go. He parked his truck down the street and I try not to let anger hit me that we have to do shit like that. Alec starts to walk away, but I reach out, and thread a finger through his belt loop. Stopping, he looks at me. He says I was the golden boy but he is. His hair's so blond and his eyes so damn blue.

"I'm sorry." The flashlight allows him to see my eyes aren't leaving his.

Alec nods. He doesn't ask what for because he knows. We've always been like that. "I know. Prove it to me though. We'll do this. We'll be friends like you said. You'll train and kick ass like you always do. Then you'll go back to school and play ball and we'll have had one last summer."

My hand falls free when he walks away, disappearing into the trees.

* * *

"Mom called me this morning." Nate looks up as I approach him out by the lake.

We've only been here a week yet he's brought up our parents at least a dozen times. I'm pretty sure I can guess what's coming next. "She called me too. I was in the shower but I haven't called her back yet."

"She asked what you've been doing since you've been here. She's worried about you. You're supposed to be training. If you don't want to play anymore, why don't you just say it?"

"I never said I didn't want to play. You don't get it." I don't know what I want. Football is all I'm good at.

"You're not acting like it. You haven't done shit since you got cleared by the doc to work out." He doesn't raise his voice but

Nate doesn't have to for people to realize he's disappointed in them. He's always done the right thing even when it's not easy. When we were younger he stuck up for a girl when her boyfriend got pushy with her, even though it turned our little town against him. That's the way he is. The repercussions don't matter as long as it's what's right.

"Not all of us can be like you." I wish like hell I could walk away from him but I can't. "Listen, I was going to ask if I could borrow your car but maybe you should take me down so I can rent my own. It would be easier."

That changes the expression on his face and he cocks his head a little. "Where are you going?"

"Do I need to ask your permission to leave? Did Mom and Dad make you my keeper while we're here?"

Nate shakes his head. "Stop being an asshole. I'm just curious."

Pushing my hands in my pockets, I groan. "I'm going to the gym...with Alec."

I can tell Nate wants to say something about that but it would make us both uncomfortable as hell. How do you talk to your brother about the guy he's into? We didn't really talk about stuff before he found out about Alec and starting now isn't something either of us wants to do.

"Keys are in the cabin on the kitchen table."

"Thanks, man." And then because I know I've been a prick to him, I add, "For everything. My head's all fucked up right now and I'm taking it out on you. You've...you've been cool about...everything." There's no doubt he would rather me be into any other guy except Alec. They have too much history because of Charlie.

"You're my brother. I'll always have your back."

"I have yours too." We bump knuckles and then I'm jogging toward the cabin. After changing into a pair of basketball shorts, tank top, and my shoes, I grab some clothes to change into after working out and pack them in a bag.

Snatching the keys off the table, I head straight to Nate's car, determined not to let myself overthink what I'm doing.

That I'm about to be alone with Alec in a way we haven't been for so long.

That for the first time since they opened my chest, since I learned I might lose the one thing that defines who I am, I'm about to take a step toward trying to get it back.

Too bad I don't know if I really want it, the way I've always known I want him.

* * *

When I pull into Alec's apartment complex he's standing outside. My grip on the steering wheel tightens, wondering if he's going to call the whole thing off.

This spark of anger, of determination I haven't felt in so damn long surges through me and I pull the car up to him, rolling down the window. "Get in."

He said we were doing this, we're doing it.

Alec opens the door and climbs into the car. "That's why I'm standing here." He pauses for a second before adding, "You thought I changed my mind?"

"No." I pull away even though I'm not sure which direction to go.

"Shut the hell up." He smiles. "You did too."

It's not like I'm going to admit it. "Where's the gym?"

I hear Alec chuckle as he clicks his seatbelt on. "Not admitting it doesn't make it less true, ya know? And we're not going to the gym."

An unexpected pang hits my gut. "I thought—"

"Have you done anything since the accident?"

The answer embarrasses me. "No."

He flips his cell over and over in his hand. "I don't know. We can go if you want to. I figured you might not want to be around a ton of people the first time. We won't have weights but I thought you might want to work into it. Maybe go for a jog or something to see what you can do."

At that my whole body goes loose. The weights I didn't realize had landed in my stomach, chest *everywhere* drop away…

"If you wanna hit the gym we can. I'm cool either way. We'll have to get you a guest pass real quick but—"

"No. We'll do that next time. Going for a jog or something sounds good for today."

Neither of us mentions my use of the words "next time."

Chapter 9

Alec

"There's a lake not too far away. It's smaller than The Village and man-made. There are some trails around it that I like. I go jogging there sometimes. People play Frisbee and stuff in this big grassy area out there too."

Brandon looks over at me and for a second I let myself really look at him. In so many ways he's so different. You wouldn't think someone could change that much in a year and a half but he has. In other ways he's the same too. The wrinkle in his forehead says he's surprised at something I said.

"You jog a lot now?"

He's already turned back to the road when I shrug. "Not a lot. Sometimes I feel like doing something but don't want to be in the gym. I like going out to the lake. It's like being home without actually having to go there." I realize how stupid that sounds since I'm less than an hour away from where I grew up. "Not that I'm all that far or anything but—"

"That doesn't matter. How far from home you go means

nothing. A person can run to the other side of the world but it doesn't mean shit if they're the same person when they get there as they were when they left. You might not have gone far from home but inside you've traveled a whole hell of a lot farther than most people...farther than me."

I can't help but scoff at that. "How? Because I've kissed a guy and then lost it when he jacked me off? I haven't done anything that matters."

Brandon flinches, his hands visibly squeezing the steering wheel. Guilt burns through me but then I'm not going to hide what happened with Logan and me, either. It could have been him. It *should* have been. The only reason another guy even had the chance to touch me is because Brandon pushed me away.

"It's a step," he bites out. "And that's not the only way you've changed."

He doesn't say anything else and I don't ask him. It doesn't take us long to get to the trails. Brandon parks off the side of the road where I point him to and we both get out of the car.

There's a bunch of rocks lined up separating the small parking area and trees and trails behind it. Three other cars are here but I know there are a few other spots too so who knows how many people are out today.

"I brought some waters in my pack. I wasn't sure if you'd have any," I tell him.

"Thanks. I figured I'd buy one at the gym." Brandon pushes up on his toes before planting his feet on the ground again, stretching out his calves. Each time he does it, the muscles constrict and I can't help watching.

God, I want to touch him so damn much. Despite his weight loss, he's still hard and strong. Looking at him, I know he's not something I'm supposed to want. There's no softness to him. No curves that guys talk so much about in the locker room. Instead he has harder edges that I don't understand how everyone can't find beautiful.

"You're staring."

A laugh tumbles out of my mouth at that, a little memory from the past jumping into the present.

"You like it when I stare at you."

Brandon grins and I know he's remembering what I am. It was our third summer together when we were teenagers. There was a big group of my friends from high school and we were all playing a game of flag football. We were skins, so no shirts. Brandon is fucking gorgeous without a shirt.

"You keep staring at me," he whispers as he walks by me.

"Sorry." I turn away. He's right. Someone's going to see and they'll know. They'll figure it out and then they'll wonder about me when we're in the locker room at school or dad will find out and I won't be a real man anymore. I'll be one of them. A fag.

I freeze when Brandon reaches out and grabs my arm. His hand is hot, and a little wet because we've been playing for hours in the heat but I don't care. I love the feel of his hands on me.

"Don't be sorry. I like your eyes on me." He looks down like he can't believe he said what he did.

"Brandon!" Charlie screams. His hand drops away and both our eyes shoot toward where Charlie's voice came from. At the same time, a football bounces off the side of Brandon's head.

Everyone starts laughing. "Pay attention, dumb-ass!" someone yells.

I laugh too because it's the thing to do and everyone starts paying attention to the game again. Trying to join in, I move to head over to the group and only get one step away when Brandon whispers…

"I like looking at you too." His words, exactly the same as what he said years ago rip me out of the memory. That easily, my cock gets hard. He's doing what he said, his eyes intense and unwavering on me. My body starts to thrum and I remember the feel of him when we were in his bed and how much I want to stroke and explore every part of him in a way I've never been able to do.

We always end up right back here but I can't even be mad this time because it's different and we're older and I'm over denying myself.

"Yeah?" I ask him.

"Yeah. You know that."

In this moment it doesn't matter that he's been a prick. It doesn't matter that nothing has really changed. I'm twenty years old. I should be screwing whoever I want and not holding on to that fantasy I used to have that one day none of it would matter and we'd find a way to be together.

Grabbing the bottom hem of my shirt, I pull it over my head. This time I know the tic in Brandon's jaw isn't from anger. His eyes trace down my chest, my abs to the six-pack that wasn't as defined when we were younger.

"Alec…" His voice comes out husky in a way I've never heard it.

There were so many times when we were teenagers where we snuck to places just like this. We'd slip off into the woods to find a spot and we'd talk and then kiss and it was so different than the girl's I'd done the same thing with. Our shirts would come off

and our bodies matched in so many ways and felt so right against each other.

He'd touch me and I'd touch him though we were too stupid and scared to try without some clothes still between us. I don't want to be stupid anymore.

"You're fucking killing me here. You just told me last night you're still pissed at me. I don't want to screw up with you. Not anymore. I'm scared as hell to do the wrong thing."

I take a step toward him. Then another. It's all Brandon needs and then he's coming toward me and backing me against the car. The metal is hot on my back but the sting doesn't touch the need rushing through me.

He grabs my sides and I grab his, wishing like hell he didn't have a shirt on either. The fabric from his top touches my stomach and then there's pressure as his body leans against me, his mouth moving toward mine.

"Holy shit that killed me!" A voice drifts from the trails in front of us. Brandon jerks away as another person laughs on the trails.

I'm breathing heavily and I'm hard as hell. Brandon must be too because he walks around the back of the car, and leans on his elbows on the hood and his hands in his hair. But I see in the smile that curves his lips and I know that even though had a helluva cock block, he wants me as much as I want

Two guys step out from one of the trails. Not paying attention to us they climb into their car and drive off.

"I love the way you make me lose my head. I never before you. I thought something was wrong when girl. Then I met you and…" He smiles. "I've been ever since."

Crazy for me. I like that. "What can I say? I'm T-shirt into the side of my backpack before

"By the looks of you I am too."

Smiling, I adjust myself. As much as I still want him, the mood is broken. He'll worry about someone else showing up and hell, I also want him to do this. He needs to start working out again. I don't want to be his excuse for not doing what we came out here to do.

"We going or not?"

"Gimme the pack. The straps will irritate you without your shirt." He reaches for me but I shake my head.

"You're wearing yours?"

"Eh. Figure I'll make it easier for you to keep your hands off me. I know what I do to you." Brandon winks and on the one hand it's like having the old Brand back but on the other, I know what he's doing. It's a lot easier to pretend nothing's changed if he doesn't have to look at the proof of it running down his chest.

I don't call him on it though. "Come on. Let's see how much warming the bench in your workout room hurt you. Hopefully you can keep up with me."

Chapter 10

Brandon

It's obvious Alec picked the easiest of the trails. A couple months ago I could have done it in my sleep and even though I'm still making it now, there's a burn in my chest and an ache in my leg muscles that would have never happened on a run this easy.

It doesn't make me stop though.

There's this war being battled inside me—the one side thrives on it. The burn is a welcome sign I'm working hard. Exercising or being on the field, those are the places I'm free. In some ways, it feels damn good to be free again but then I have that other side mocking me. It's telling me this should be easier than it is and what if I can't get past it? What if I can't work up to where I need to be?

And what if I can? I'm scared to lose my level of physicality and afraid to get it back too. Then I have no choice but to keep lying to everyone and living football because if I don't, who the fuck am I?

"Brand?" Alec keeps pace beside me.

"Don't. Don't ask if I'm okay." My voice is breathless. The thought of Alec thinking he needs to question me on something this basic makes me push harder—my legs move faster.

"Can I ask if you want to go to the left or the right up at the V?"

Turning my head, I look at him, with this big, cheesy grin, his blond hair slightly sweat tinged, though not as much as mine. We don't break pace as I reach over and shove him. "Fucker."

Alec stumbles a little but doesn't fall. "Just checking...Since I'm not allowed to ask you certain things there must be a script I don't know about." We both know left or right wasn't what he was originally going to ask.

"Wherever you go, I'll follow you."

The look on his face changes, this sort of sadness creeping in. It kills me when he looks like that. It's not him. He's always happy and I'm not sure what caused the switch.

"I wish that was true," he says.

Alec veers off to the right. My feet tangle a little but I keep on them, and go with him, following him in the way I can, wishing the same damn thing he is.

After a while, we loop around and jog back to the car. The longer we go the more I have to slow down but I refuse to let myself stop. It's a simple fucking jog. I'm a football player. There's no way I can't do this.

When we get back to the car, I drop against it. Alec opens his pack and takes a drink of the last water bottle before handing it to me.

I down the whole thing.

"I gotta ask, man, but it's because I'm worried. You feel okay? I mean, I know you're tired because you have to build your stamina and stuff back up but…you don't feel anything different do you? With your heart?"

I hate that he's asking me but I'm honored by it too. I'd rather look weak in front of anyone in the fucking world than him…but he's also the only place I feel comfortable enough to let my guard down. It's exhausting, always feeling so conflicted around him.

"I'm good. It's not really like that. I mean, it's not a real heart condition. But yeah, I'm good. Just to be sure I had a couple monitored workout sessions back home. No problems." And those were the only times I really did workout. I'm sure he knows that though.

Alec nods and goes to walk around to the other side of the car but on reflex, I reach up and rest my hand on the back of his neck before he can go. "Thanks for asking. And for taking me today."

He nods and I rub my thumb through the wet hair at the nape of his neck before pulling away.

"We can keep it up if you want. Your body is used to being active, Brand. We can do it every day."

The heaviness in my shoulders starts to slip away. I could see us doing that. We used to run around doing shit every day all summer. When I think about being with Alec, that fist doesn't tighten around my gut like it does every time I tried to get back into shape alone. It's like the way we used to be. Like he said last night…just that easily we're us.

"The NFL has always been your plan. You can't do that if you don't start training again."

I feel my lips tug into a smile. A big smile that I'm sure looks cheesy.

"What are you smiling at, dumb-ass?" Alec pushes at my shoulder.

"You didn't say it's been my dream. You said it's my plan." Dream? Plan? The word in a way has the same meaning for me.

"That's because I know you."

My fingers flex, begging to touch him. My mind starts spinning, wanting to talk to him. To pretend none of that shit of the past happened but all of the good did. "Come on. Let's go back to your place."

The drive is quick and I don't let myself think too much on the way there. I know I can get shot down, I know he might have plans or maybe that fucker Logan is coming over, all of which would serve me right but I don't let it stop me from voicing what I want. "I'm not ready to go back. I just want to chill with you. Will you let me come up?"

"Don't pretend you don't know the answer to that. Come on. I have burgers and a grill on my patio. We can barbecue or something."

He gets out of the car and then I do the same. "Hell no. You're not touching the grill. Remember when we went camping? That shit looked like charcoal when you finished with it."

"Screw you. I was like five."

After grabbing my bag out of the backseat, I slam the door. "You were seventeen."

Alec gets a look on his face that tells me he's up to something. "A guy can learn a lot between then and now. Gets better at a lot of things too."

Holy shit, he's going to fucking kill me. "You do that a whole hell of a lot more than you used to." It's sexy as hell too.

Alec winks.

His apartment complex is a little older but nice. We take the concrete steps up to his place on the second floor. I wait as Alec opens the door, still shocked that we're here. After everything we're... not together again, if what we were you could consider that. We thought of ourselves that way. Now we're probably too old to think that way. Especially since we haven't really talked about anything, and because regardless, I'll be back in Ohio in August. Back to being number forty-three.

Alec throws his keys on the table and sets the backpack on one of the chairs. He's still not wearing a shirt, corded muscles running the length of his arms but they're nothing compared to the rest of him. He's more lithe than I am.

"I stink. You cool if I take a quick shower? You can use it after me."

I set my bag on the table. "Yeah. No problem. Wasn't sure how much longer I could deal with the smell anyway."

"Ha ha. You got jokes now?"

"I've always had them." I step closer to him. "I make you laugh."

Alec rolls his eyes. "I'm going now. Make yourself at home, yeah?"

When he leaves, I pull my cell out of my pocket and call my brother. It's already six and I'm hoping like hell he and Charlie don't need the car back right now.

"Hey." Nate answers on the third ring. "What's up?"

"Do you need your car back right away?" I feel like a loser having to borrow his vehicle—like I'm asking permission to be out.

"No, we're just chillin' here. Charlotte wants to go out with her telescope tonight." She's in school for astronomy.

"So you're cool if I keep it a while longer?" It's weird as hell talking to him when he's knows I'm with Alec. When Nate found out about us, it was only a couple months before I broke things off with him. Nate and Charlie were heading back to Virginia from New York so even though he knows everything, there's only been a few times when Alec and I have been together with Nate in the know—the night he first found out about us and Mom went into early labor with Joshua, when Alec came after my heart surgery, and now.

"Keep it as long as you want!" Charlie yells, obviously right next to Nate and listening in.

I roll my eyes. "Thanks."

"You're welcome!" Charlie replies.

Laughing, I say, "You wanna put her on the phone or what, man?"

"She's already texting Alec."

"It's not...we're not..." Excuses automatically start trying to fall out of my mouth but I fight to hold them back. *This is my brother. He knows. It's okay.* And hell, it feels good for someone to know. To be able to say I'm staying with Alec the way I've always envied Nate can do with Charlie.

But Charlie is his...Alec isn't mine.

Tired of overthinking things, I push all my thoughts aside. This is Nate. "We went for a jog and now we're going to grill some burgers or something. It's not what you think. I mean, we're friends. I have training in August."

My brother pauses and I automatically wonder if I grossed him out. If he doesn't want me to talk to him about Alec at all.

"That's six weeks away, bro. Every summer Charlie and I knew we'd have to say good-bye but that didn't stop us from taking advantage of the time we had. You...you deserve a little bit of happiness. You both do."

I don't know what makes me do it—how I find the words. Maybe I'm tired of holding it all in or maybe it's what Nate said or all the things Alec and I have talked about. I lean against Alec's kitchen table and speak. "I want to be happy. I just...I want to just *be*. That probably doesn't make any fucking sense but…I want to be normal." A deep breath leaves my lungs. "With him."

"Then do it. Whatever you have to do or however you have to do it. Fucking find a way. You know we'll always be there for you, no matter what. Mom and Dad will too."

A click sounds from down the hallway, before Alec rounds the corner out of the bathroom. He shakes his head and I watch as his blond hair flies up before settling messily on his head. He's wearing a pair of red basketball shorts, still without a shirt.

And he is so fucking gorgeous.

"I want him happy too…" I whisper. "I gotta go. I'll see you soon." Before Nate replies, I click end on the call.

"There's towels in the cabinet by the sink. Sometimes the nob sticks but—" Alec stops dead, studying me—dissecting me as though he sees the thoughts in my mind as I form them. "What?"

My whole body is hyped up like someone injected adrenaline into me. I want nothing more than to push him against the wall. To take his mouth and whatever else he would give me, so at least once, he could fully be mine.

But that's always what I do when it comes to him, isn't it? I broke up with him because it was better for me. Hurting him isn't an option again.

"Nothing." I step away from the table. "Talked to Nate. You know how he can be."

"Yeah. I used to dream about kicking his ass every summer. I might not have really been in love with Charlie like everyone thought, but I didn't think he was good for her either."

He steps around me, no clue that I really don't want to talk about Charlie, Nate, or anyone else. I just want him.

"Like I said, sometimes the faucet sticks on the shower. Pull it hard and it'll come on." Alec goes into the kitchen and opens the fridge.

"Okay." As much as I hate it, all I can think is maybe that's a sign for me to relax. Before I say anything to him—when really I don't even know where in the hell to start—I need to cool off. A cold shower is the best place I can think to start.

Chapter 11

Alec

By the time Brandon gets out of the shower, I'm sitting in one of the two chairs on my balcony. It's small so there's not a lot of room. My grill is in the right corner, and then the two chairs on the other side, no more than five feet away from the barbecue. The charcoal just turned gray enough for me to put the burgers on.

There's beer left from when Logan was here so before Brand comes out, I call through the sliding screen door, "There's beer in the fridge if you want one."

"Thanks." His words drift through the house hitting me with this ridiculous sense of shock that Brandon Chase is in my apartment right now. When he called things off, it was like someone carved my heart out of my chest. Yeah, dramatic but true. I knew, when he had the balls to do that, I *knew* we were done.

And we still are. That knowledge is in the back of my head. We don't have a future. I know Brandon. He's going to work his ass off and he'll play ball again and he won't ever come out to his team.

And yet, he's here and I'm still trying to wrap my head around the fact.

When the screen squeaks behind me, I lean forward so Brandon can get past me to sit in the other chair, before putting my feet up on the railing. It's a battle to resist the urge to glance over at him and see what he's wearing.

"Burgers on?" Out of the corner of my eye, I see him take a drink of beer.

"Yep. I got my own special seasoning too. They'll kick ass and then you'll regret ever talking shit to me about grilling."

Brandon laughs, before nudging my arm. "I was teasing you. You can't take a joke anymore?"

This time, I don't stop myself from looking over. His brown eyes are on me, with what I've always thought looks like gold highlights in them. "I can take it."

Those highlights look like they were lit on fire. "You're doing that shit on purpose."

"What?" I tease.

"Fuck you. You're a guy. You know exactly how my head automatically took that."

At that, I laugh. "Sorry if your *head* can't handle it." My eyes dart to his crotch before I stand, ready to flip the food. Brandon reaches his hand out but before he makes contact with my arm, he seems to realize what he's doing and drops it.

If we'd been inside, he would have pulled me to him. Those first summers we spent together the touches were less frequent, more nervous. But at the end, when we managed to sneak away so it was only the two of us, we weren't afraid to put our hands on each other.

I wonder if it's like that for everyone. If people in love want to feel the other person all the time like we did.

Hell, maybe it didn't mean anything and we were just horny but also too chicken shit to do much about it.

After flipping the burgers I sit back down next to him. The sun's getting lower but it's still hot out. Brand's wearing another T-shirt and shorts that hang below his knees.

"Are you embarrassed by your scar?" I ask him.

"No." He takes a drink of his beer. "You know me better than that. I'm not that superficial." Another drink. "I don't like to look at it. It reminds me of everything—that I could have died, that I'm scrawny as hell now—"

"You're not scrawny."

"For me, I am. And that I have to work up to do shit I used to do easily. That I could lose football."

"Would you really hate to lose it?" As soon as the question comes out, I know it's stupid.

"Fuck yeah. Even you would hate to lose it. That means you don't have a choice. That something was taken away from you. No matter what, Al, you know there's a part of me who loves to play."

And that's true. It's his passion.

"But you don't feel like it's a game you're playing, you think it defines you. I also know as much as you love the game, you hate that piece of it."

"It's the only thing I've ever been good at." He sighs.

That's a lie. He was good at being with me. "What else have you tried?" Pushing to my feet, I say, "I'll be right back."

Inside I pull out the buns before grabbing the tomato slices out of the fridge. There are a few hamburger pickles in a jar so I set them on the counter too, followed by the mustard and mayo.

Because dishes suck, I pick a few paper plates off the stack and then head back outside. "Forty-five seconds and they'll be ready to pull off."

Brandon huffs. "Got it down to the seconds now, huh?"

"Watch and see." When the time is up, I raise the lid off the grill and put the burgers on the plate. "Wait till you taste these."

Brandon reaches around me and slides the screen open for me.

"Thanks," I mumble before leading the way inside. We make our burgers in the kitchen. I don't have anything except potato chips to go with them, so I take those out and Brandon nods his head toward them, waiting for me to take a handful out before he does.

"I'll grab you another beer." He opens the fridge and takes two out and then we're on the balcony again.

There's no table but neither of us hesitates to put the plates on our laps. Like an idiot, I wait for him to take a bite before I eat. After he swallows I raise an eyebrow at him and Brandon says, "Okay, so you *might* be able to barbecue now."

"That's what I thought." I lean back into the chair to start eating, and I can't help but feel...content.

* * *

It's dark out now, the porch light above us making it so we can see. We've been out here for hours, the only thing either of us has gone inside for is something to drink, take a piss or when I grabbed a shirt to keep the mosquitoes from eating me alive.

We've talked about everything and nothing too. Nothing big, and everything small but the conversation has hardly stopped the whole time. We've always been like that. I wonder if it's because we keep one of the most important pieces of ourselves quiet from the world, so we can't help but want to talk about everything when we're together.

There's a slight lull in the conversation now and I can't stop thinking of the fact that we haven't been like this in years. When he goes back to Ohio, we'll never be like this again.

We were together and then the next thing I knew he forced me to walk away from him. One day he was fine and the next they'd cut his chest open to do surgery on his heart. It makes you think. Makes you realize how fast shit changes.

"I don't want to spend my summer working with my dad, man. I know that's messed up but I don't."

"Screw that. It's not fucked up. I hate the way he is with you."

I shrug even though I'm not sure if he's looking at me. My eyes are forward, looking at the stars Charlie loves so much. "It's really not that bad. I know he loves me. He's not abusive...just ignorant and outspoken, which don't go well together."

Brandon doesn't say anything, so I continue. "That's what stresses me out. I know he loves me. I'm his son and we've always been close. It's just the older I got, when I started to realize I was gay, I noticed more things about him I hated. I did more things he didn't understand. The thing is..." I take a deep breath. "I'm not going to keep doing this, ya know? I don't want to hide forever. I'm not saying I'll be ready to come out tomorrow but I know it will be soon and when I do, I know he really will hate me. I'm scared the more I'm around him, the more I'll think about that. I'm afraid I'll start to hate him and I'm not ready for that to happen yet."

"Shit...I'm sorry."

Out of the corner of my eye, Brandon moves. I think he's switching positions but then I feel his slightly callused hand on the back of my neck. It's dark out, and my balcony is closed off enough that no one can really see us. It feels so damn good to have him reach over and touch me without holding back because he wants to be there for me.

"You are so fucking brave. Do you know that? So brave. And he won't hate you, Al. How could anyone hate you?"

I chuckle a little, before I let my eyes drift closed. I take a couple deep breaths before I open them again, and try to lighten the mood. "Your brother hated me."

"That's because he thought you wanted to fuck Charlie."

"Yeah I guess it changes things now that he knows I really want to fuck his brother."

Brandon groans, his grip tightening on my neck, and then it's gone and I'm pissed because I think he's pulling back. He grabs my arm when he stands. I go easily with him but then jerk free from his hold. "Chill the hell out. No one heard me. You didn't have to pull me up."

Roughly, I push the screen door open and go inside. White-hot anger burns a hole through me. What was I thinking that I could be honest with him? That he wouldn't find a way to freak out.

The glass door slams behind me. "Did you mean it?" Brandon bites out.

Oh…shit. At that I whip around to face him. "Is that really a question?"

I see it in his eyes—see him want to laugh at what I said but his lips don't move. His chest heaves in and out. Hell, I think mine is too.

"Last night I tried to kiss you and you told me you were still pissed."

"Part of me still is but that doesn't mean I don't want you. You remember what you said to me? That you wanted some part of me. You don't think I want whatever I can have of you too? Come on, Brand. You're not stupid."

My feelings are this weird jumble of…well, fucked up. Is

there a part of me who's scared to screw around with him? Yeah. I know I'm gay but doing more than simple touching or kissing, that means there's no going back. I really am gay. I think that's part of the reason I freaked with Logan but that doesn't mean I'm not horny as hell. No guy wants to be a twenty-year-old virgin. With him it's a million times stronger, this constant buzz zipping around under my skin just because it's *Brandon*. Everything is stronger with him.

He's still standing there, chest surging in out and, his eyes hard on me.

"You know what? Never mind. I—" My words are cut off by his lips crushing mine. It's quick, urgent, desperate and our teeth clink together. But then my lips part and he pushes his tongue inside and I'm trying to do the same to him.

Our mouths battle. His hands cup either side of my face as I push mine up under his shirt, wanting to feel him—flesh-covered steel.

Brandon pushes forward and I stumble backward. My foot tangles on the leg of the coffee table and I almost fall, but then Brandon's pushing it out of the way with his foot. Back... back...back, he continues moving forward, making me fall but the couch catches me, Brandon coming down on top of me.

He laughs and I can't help but do the same.

"Shit. I'm sorry. Didn't want you to change your mind." He kisses the corner of my mouth, before whispering, "Please don't change your mind." A kiss to the other side. "I want you so much."

My dick is so hard I feel like I'm going to explode. But yeah... it's more than that. "I want you too."

This time, it's my mouth pushing against his. My tongue parting his lips. I lean forward and Brandon seems to read my mind, pushing up too. Our mouths don't part. He has one knee on the couch. His other leg is on the opposite side of me, his foot on the floor like he's straddling me but still able to hold himself up. He's slightly sitting on me. When I have enough room between myself and the couch, I pull my mouth off his. Brandon pushes my hands out of the way when I start to go for my shirt, and then he's lifting it and pulling it over my head.

He doesn't hesitate to go for his next, throwing it somewhere on the ground before he's kissing me again.

This time I purposely fall back and he's comes down right on top of me, the hot skin of his chest against mine.

Brandon's mouth slides down my neck, and each time he moves, I feel the roughness of his scar, reminding me what happened.

I squeeze him tighter, my hand in his hair and then his tongue runs up the side of my neck. "I love the taste of your skin."

My cock jerks. "Holy shit. Don't say stuff like that or I'm going to embarrass myself."

He just chuckles and then kisses me again, his tongue sweeping my mouth.

I move my hips and when I do, my dick brushes against his. Brandon jerks his mouth away, "Oh fuck," huskily comes out of his mouth; at the same time, I hiss.

So close. I'm already so damn close.

Brandon's bottom half is flat against mine. One of his arms is holding him up a little, making the muscles move and constrict and it's so hot.

He smiles down at me and it makes more lust shoot through me. He's so gorgeous and he looks…happy.

And then he's moving. Each time he nudges his hips into me, our cocks rub together and it's like the epicenter of everything I feel. It tells my body it's the most incredible thing that's ever happened and I swear I feel that touch everywhere.

Pulling him toward me, I open my mouth when his comes down on mine again. My hips are matching his rhythm now, each of us moving together, rubbing each other off.

I run my hand down his back. His muscles working and he's thrusting harder each time. I want to slow down, want to hold it back because I really need this feeling to last forever.

Brandon moves again, his cock thrusting against mine, right as he nips at my bottom lip.

"Oh fuck." I can't stop the orgasm from slamming into me.

In. My. Shorts.

Then Brandon's tensing over me mumbling something that sounds like it's a different language or some shit and I know he just lost it too.

We're both sweaty and he lets himself drop down onto me. He's heavy but there's nothing in me that would ask him to move. The weight feels good. Feels right.

His breath is in my ear, neither of us talking before he pants, "You losing it like that wasn't embarrassing. It was fucking hot."

And he's right but hell, that whole thing couldn't have lasted more than maybe five minutes.

Still… "It was incredible."

Brandon leans up a little. Touches my hair. Quickly presses his lips to mine. "It was perfect."

Chapter 12

Brandon

Alec grins up at me and I'm ready to start all over again. It wouldn't take much at all for me to get it up, I don't think.

"You're easy." He winks.

"You don't even know the half of it." I wish like hell I didn't have to but I sit up. "Do you have something I can wear?" The other clothes I have are all sweaty from our jog.

Alec moves his legs around me and stands up. "Yeah. Changing sounds good."

I follow him down the hall and to his room. Alec flips on the light. There's a queen bed across the room with a black comforter. He walks over to the dark oak dresser, while I go to the table by his bedside. There's a lamp there, and an iPod, and a picture of him with Charlie when they were little.

He has a shelf on the other wall with old football trophies on it and a picture of him with his varsity team. The table on the other side of his bed has a laptop on it, even though there's a desk in one of the corners too. It has books and papers on it, I'm assuming from school.

"Brand."

Turning my head, I look at him just in time to catch a pair of shorts he tosses at me. "Thanks." I don't know why I'm so interested in his room. It's just…him. This is where he comes to be him where most people don't usually go.

"I'll be right back." He heads into the bathroom and closes the door. I walk over to his dresser next. As much as I like looking around, I'm hoping he hurries so I can clean up too.

There's one of those clear paperweights with an image inside. It's a football player. He has a bottle of cologne and deodorant. And then sitting there is a cheap keychain. I know because I bought it for three bucks when him and Charlie came to New York the fourth summer I knew him. It was a joke, really. We saw it when I was showing him around the city and we both laughed at how cheesy it was but I bought it anyway and when we left the store, I told him he dropped something and handed it to him.

NEW YORK LOVES YOU!

Which really is lame. At the time it was funny. But he kept it.

Picking it up, I run my thumb over the blue letters.

The bathroom door opens. "You're up. Throw your clothes in the washer when you're done."

I set it down before he sees me holding it and head toward the door. "Thanks."

Alec nods his head toward another door. "The washer's right here."

"Cool. Thanks." Without looking at him, I duck into the bathroom and close the door. After taking off my shorts and boxer-briefs, I grab a washcloth and clean up before I take a quick piss, wash my hands, and pull on the shorts Alec gave me, free ballin' it. Then I go out and toss everything in the washer, turn it on, and then look back in Alec's room. He's lying on the bed, one of his legs out straight, the other bent at the knee while he's looking at his phone.

The computer's on next to his bed, ESPN playing.

"So what are you gonna do? About your dad and work and stuff."

He looks over at me. "I don't know. I have a little money saved but not a ton. What are you going to do about working out? You know you gotta do it, man. Even if something crazy happened and you decided not to play. You love it too much not to."

Feeling like an idiot standing in the middle of his bedroom, I walk over and sit right next to him. Alec has to scoot over a little but doesn't go far enough away that our sides aren't still touching.

"I know…Even today. I was pissed out there but it felt awesome too. I think…I think I'm ready to start getting serious about it. I don't have that long before camp."

He nods. "Then we'll do it. Someone's gotta keep you in line. I don't think anyone else but me could handle you."

"I don't want to do it with anyone but you, but again…what about work? And your dad?"

"I'll help him a day or so a week. He'll think it's my days off. They don't have to know I lost my job."

Leaning forward, I cover his mouth with mine. He tastes a little like mint, as my tongue strokes his. He must have brushed his teeth while he was in the bathroom and I wish I would've thought to at least finger brush. After I pull away, I climb in behind Alec, my head on the pillows next to his. "I could help… with bills or whatever—"

"No. Screw that. You're not paying my bills, Brand."

"It's not a big deal." But I know it is. I wouldn't let him pay for my stuff either.

"Don't bullshit me."

Pausing, I run the words over in my head a million times, wondering if I should say them but knowing I will anyway. After tonight, I'm not ready to walk away from him yet—not that I ever am. But it also has to be his call. I'm the one who didn't give him a say when I walked away, he deserves this one. "What about us?" Rolling over, I lean up on my elbow and look down at him.

There's a tiny scar by his left nipple that I don't remember noticing before. I was right about his abs, each muscle defined.

"Before I thought you were going to be a prick when you grabbed me on the porch, I was going to talk to you about that." But then he pauses. I wait for him to speak again, letting Alec run the show. "When you came here to tell me it was over—"

The bottom drops out of my gut.

"I didn't say anything. I know I probably couldn't have changed your mind but I could have fought a little harder. You could have died in that accident and I would have regretted it forever. With Logan—"

"Argh. Do we really have to talk about him?"

"He's my friend, Brand. And yeah, we do. When he tried to hook up with me, I freaked out. I regretted it after. It's not that I really wanted him all that much but enough that I shouldn't have kicked him out. It shouldn't be like that. I'm tired of letting shit pass me by. There's never been anything I've wanted like I want you. I don't want you to be another regret. Not again."

My heart is going a million miles an hour but I don't care. All I can focus on is him.

"So yeah...I want it this time. We both know what it is now. I know you're leaving and you know you're leaving but you're here now. So I say we do it. We just fucking pretend, and we be happy and when it's time, we man up and say good-bye. Until then we enjoy ourselves and you train and…"

I don't want to, don't ever want to tell him good-bye. That's not how I reply though. "It's gonna get tough without a car. I can't keep borrowing Nate and Charlie's. And there's no gym in Lakeland Village. If I'm going to train to get back on the football field, I need to be by the gym."

Alec looks up at me. "I have a spare room. It's the right thing to do…letting you stay here. I mean, for your football career and all."

My answer is cupping his cheek with my hand and then leaning down to kiss him. Alec moans into my mouth and it's so fucking hot, I immediately get hard again.

"Look at you. Who knew Brandon Chase was so romantic. You better take me out and kick my ass on the football field so I know you're still a man. I'm not into girls, ya know."

I shove him and Alec rolls over, laughing. "Fuck you. I'll kick your ass right here if you say that again." And then because I knew he won't expect it, I put my mouth next to his ear. "That's not all I'll do to it either."

He's lying on his stomach now, but lifts his head and faces me. "Point made. I know exactly who you are."

A buzz comes from the hallway screaming at us that the washer is done. Alec goes to get up, but I put a hand on his back. "I got it."

It's one of those stackable ones so the dryer's right above the washer. I toss the clothes and stuff in before turning it on. The lights are still on in the living room, so I go in there, make sure the doors are locked and then turn everything off. Now I get to be the guy who's at home here.

My body is all primed on the way back to the room. It's not

like this is the first time Alec and I have spent nights in bed together but we're on a different level now than we were before.

The hallway's dark as I make my way down it. Before I even get to his door, I see Alec, laid out on his stomach, one of his legs bent and an arm thrown up above his head.

I scratch the scar running up the middle of my bare chest, though I'm not sure why. It didn't even itch.

Still, after all the shit we've been through, I love him. And I have six weeks with him.

I hit the light before walking over and, shutting the laptop down before getting into bed. Lying on my side, I wrap an arm around Alec's waist and go to sleep.

* * *

My eyes just sort of pop open for no reason. The room's still dark and I'm guessing it's an hour or two before the sun comes up. Alec's still passed out pretty much in the same position he was in when he fell asleep, except he's turned toward me now instead of the other direction.

My hand twitches with the urge to touch him. To run my finger down the middle of his back, just to feel his skin, and make sure he's really here. I shake my head, embarrassed of my own thoughts—of how sappy I am when it comes to him.

"I am such a fucking idiot," I mumble, with a smile on my face.

Even though I don't want to, I slip out of the bed. I take a quick leak before rinsing my mouth out with some mouthwash, which is all I can do until I get back to The Village to brush my teeth.

After grabbing my clothes from the dryer, I change quickly before checking the time to see it's four a.m.

Quietly I go back into Alec's room, and kneel on the floor next to him. Brushing my fingers over his shoulder blade, I whisper, "Hey."

He moans and for some reason it shoots straight to my crotch, instantly making me hard again.

"I'm going to go, Al. I want to get Nate's car back to him. And talk to him…you know, about everything."

He groans again before rolling over to look at me, his eyes fluttering. I tilt my cell the other direction so the light isn't right in his eyes.

"You're still coming back? Didn't expect that." His words are slurred.

I hate that he has every right to doubt me. "Yeah. I'm coming back. I meant what I said."

"Hold up a sec. I'll get dressed and go with you." He moves but I put my hand on his back again.

"No. It's early. Go back to bed. If anyone sees, they'll wonder why you came with me at four thirty in the morning."

"Good point." His eyes are closed, already falling asleep again.

"I'll text you later, when I have all my shit together and you can come get me. Or I can have Nate bring me back if you want."

"I'll come," tumbles out of his mouth.

I think he'd always come for me. "I know." Leaning forward, I kiss the corner of his mouth before pushing to my feet and sneaking out of the room.

The whole drive back to the cabins I can't stop thinking about how easy and natural last night was.

How right it felt. If we could keep locked away like that, we'd always be happy.

When I get back to the cabins, my plan is to sneak in as quietly as I can. It's not as if Nate and Charlie don't know where I

was or that I didn't come home last night but I also don't want
to go make a big deal of it either. When I go inside, Nate's passed
out on the couch.

He jumps up the second the door closes, obviously not as
sound a sleeper as Alec.

"Did you really try to stay up waiting for me?" It surprises me
when I smile.

He rubs his eyes. "When you say it like that it sounds a little
creepy but…" He shrugs. "I was worried about you."

Translation: He thought I would freak out, bail on Alec, and
then need someone to talk to. Talk about making me feel weak
as hell.

"Nothing to worry about. Everything's good." Better than
good. "I'd still be there if I didn't want to make sure I got your
car back to you." I'm tired of feeling weak.

I hid being with Alec, pretty much for four years. I've always
hid who I was. I talked shit about dating girls and sleeping with
girls, trying to cover the fact that I was really with him. For once,
I just… want it to feel normal. Want to treat our relationship like
anyone else would.

"I know you and Charlie probably want your space, so I'm
gonna stay with Alec for the rest of the summer." My back is to
him, as I go the fridge and open it. I have the orange juice out and
a cup half filled when Nate finally replies.

"No shit?"

I shrug before taking a drink. "Why not? He has the space
and there's a gym close by. He's going to start training with me
every day."

Nate gets up and walks into the kitchen. "Are you guys…?"
Nate doesn't finish his sentence.

"Are we really going to talk about this, man? And not just

because he's a guy. It's not like I sit around talking to you about Charlie."

"A long time ago you asked me if I loved her."

I ignore him.

"Do you trust anyone?" he asks, making me feel even worse than I already do. I always tell myself I'm going to trust him more, get closer to him. He tried like hell to be there for me when he found out about Alec.

"I trust you...and I trust him." I shrug. "I've always loved him, but that doesn't change how things are. We're just gonna chill. We both want to spend these last few weeks together and then we're really going to end it for good."

He frowns, obviously not approving.

"That reminds me, he doesn't want anyone here to know about his job, okay? Can you make sure Charlie doesn't tell either? He doesn't want to have to spend every day here with his dad."

Nate nods. I hit him on the arm. "Thanks, man." Turning, I head toward my room.

"I hope you know what you're doing, bro." His voice is serious.

I don't turn around. *I hope I do too.*

Chapter 13

Alec

My cell rings in the morning. Without looking, I know who it is. Grabbing it, I see it's 10:00 a.m. and that I'm right, it's Charlie. I almost don't answer but I know her and she won't stop trying so I might as well deal with it now.

"What?"

"Well hello to you too." I wait for her to continue because there's no stopping her anyway. "Brandon stayed the night at your house, Alec. That's pretty huge for you guys."

"I love you, Charlie, but you're crazy if you think I'm talking to you about this."

She sighs. "I had a feeling you'd say that. Nate said Brandon's coming back to stay with you."

"Makes sense. The gym's right here. I have an extra room."

"And we both know that has nothing to do with it."

Instead of replying to that, I change the subject. "You didn't say anything about my job, right?"

"No...It never came up and Brandon told Nate this morning not to mention it."

"Cool." I sit up in bed, and scratch my chest. He's really doing it. Coming to stay here with me. For six weeks.

"I know you don't want to talk about it but can I ask you one question? I'm worried about you."

Damn it. This is the last thing I want to deal with it. "One question as long as you keep it to yourself if you don't like my answer."

"Alec—"

"I'm serious, Charlie. I'm not walking away from this."

"Okay then, that's my question. What's 'this'? Are you guys back together? Are you trying to make this work?"

A laugh falls out of my mouth. "That's more than one question."

"And you're not answering on purpose! Alec...I love Brandon, but you're my priority. I need to make sure you're going to be okay."

Standing up, I walk into my living room, my shirt still on the floor from last night. Holy shit that was hot.

"Alec?"

I collapse onto the couch and put my feet on the coffee table. "You're the one who called me when he was hurt, Charlie. Now you're worried I'm spending time with him?"

"I'm concerned that he's moving in with you!" she shouts.

It's obvious now that I shouldn't have answered the phone. "Listen, I know you're worried but I'm doing this. I'm doing it for *me*. Too much passes me by and I'm not gonna let him and this summer be one of them, okay? I know exactly what's going to happen this time. He's leaving for school in August and he'll go into the draft and the NFL. That'll be the end of it." It doesn't mean I like knowing where we'll end up but I need this time too.

"I just don't get what the rush is, ya know?"

"Rush?" We've been playing this game with each other for five years. "I'm not even going to reply to that."

She pauses, which is something she doesn't usually do. There's more she wants but finally settles on, "I know he loves you but that won't stop you from getting hurt. You know I want you guys together, Alec. I always have. Be careful, okay?"

Frustrated, I rub a hand over my face. We're just having fun. Both of us deserve that. "It'll be fine, Charlie. I know what I'm doing." Knowing will help me accept it when Brand leaves.

* * *

Brandon waited until my dad was gone to text me but of course he's back by the time I get there to pick Brand up. My whole body is in knots like it is every time I see him. The older I get the more the knots multiply and the tighter they get.

He might not believe Brandon's renting my spare room. He might question it. I don't want him to call me a pussy...to call me a fag.

The fact is, it'll happen soon enough. I have zero doubts how things will go down when I tell him I'm gay, but damned if I want it to ruin the rest of the summer. All I want right now is the next six weeks.

"What are you doing here?" He wipes the sweat from his forehead but there's a smile on his face. Dad and I have always spent a lot of time together. He's what made me start loving football but everything else he knows about me is a lie.

"I switched shifts with one of the guys at work."

Leaves crackle and a twig breaks, and I know Brand must be walking up to us.

"So you came to help your old man out? You're a hard worker just like your dad, kid."

You wouldn't be saying that if you knew. You wouldn't want a queer like me to be anything like you.

"Still a little soft sometimes. I was playing college ball and had three girlfriends at the same time when I was your age. You got a lot of catching up to do." He laughs and I laugh too because that's just what I do. I definitely don't remind him that he got hurt halfway through his freshman year, dropped out and came back home to marry Mom. He always thought Charlie would be to me what Mom is to him—and I guess I did too.

As soon as he reaches us, Brandon steps right up beside me.

"Maybe I've already started catching up. I had a whole hell of a lot of fun last night."

Brandon stiffens next to me. Dad grabs me, playfully putting me in a headlock while giving me a noogie. "That's my boy."

I make myself laugh again before pushing him away. "Get off. I didn't come to help either. I came to get Brandon. He's going to start training again so he can get in shape for senior year. It'll be a lot easier for him in town with the gym right there."

"No shit?" Dad beams at Brandon, the way he never really looked at me. I was always good at football but he never pushed it on me, even though he'd tried to leave Lakeland Village to play. When I was young, I didn't really get it. When I got older I realized it's because he didn't think I could do it. He never expected me to go all the way. In a lot of ways that was perfect because I didn't want to leave. If I stayed here it would be easy to pretend I was the Alec everyone thought I was. I'd marry my best friend and be normal. Things didn't work out that way.

"Yeah." There's a harsh edge to Brandon's voice and he crosses his arms. Dad doesn't seem to notice.

"Good for you!" Dad replies to him.

"Alec's helping me train. He kicks my ass out there."

"When you get back tonight, we'll have to swap college stories."

Half a season. You only played for half a fucking season.

"I won't be back tonight. I left my car in New York and since I'm going to be at the gym so much, I asked Alec if I could rent his spare room for a few weeks."

Dad's hand comes down on my shoulder. "Good for you. That's a nice thing for you to do for your friend."

"Thanks." His hand on me is like a disease—one that wants into my blood so it can spread quickly. It makes me step away.

"Can you help me get my shit?" Brandon's already walking away before the last word leaves his mouth.

"Get out of here. I'll catch you guys later. Good luck, Brandon!" Dad shouts, as I jog after Brand.

The second we get in the cabin, he slams the door. "Fucking-A it kills me not to knock him out."

"He doesn't mean to be a dick, Brand. He doesn't get it." The smaller room is right off the living room so I head to it, figuring that must be where he's staying.

"That doesn't make it okay." He's following behind me.

"And I'm also not a girl. I don't need you to defend me." The bedroom door clicks closed behind him.

"Hey. That's not what I meant."

When I turn to face him, he steps up to me, no more than a couple inches between us. Brandon's eyes dart to the window, where he must find the blinds closed because he hooks a finger under my chin and tilts my head up. "I know exactly who you are."

His lips brush mine and it's way too slow and soft for me. I slip my tongue between his lips and he sucks it into his mouth, before letting it go again. I sweep his mouth before retreating and then it's his tongue doing the exploring.

"I like the feel of this." With this thumb he rubs the stubble on my face.

"You don't need to give me compliments to screw me."

Brandon laughs. "It used to be me who always had something sarcastic to say. I need to catch up."

I don't get how his team or his friends don't get how he's changed. Or maybe he just fakes it better around them then he does me. "I'm sure you will. I'll be telling you to shut up and leave me alone in no time."

"Bastard." He pushes me away. "Come on. Let's get my stuff and get out of here. I'm ready to hit the gym."

And there he is. The old Brandon is already coming back.

* * *

A couple hours later I'm looking down at Brandon as he lies on the bench. The muscles in his arms rock solid as he slowly pushes the bar up.

"Come on, Brand. You got this." I keep myself ready in case I have to help him. The gym is older and although they do have some newer equipment, there are a lot of free weights too.

He lowers the bench press bar. "I know."

I smirk at him. There's a gleam of sweat on him as his muscles work. His face flushed and damned if it's not sexy. "Already turning into a cocky bastard again."

"I can't help it if I'm good." The bar goes up again but slower this time.

"Two more. Stop talking."

I watch for any sign that he needs me. I hate it because I know he wants this—he needs it but it's scary as hell too. Yeah, his doctor cleared him but what if something goes wrong? I won't insult him by letting him see my fear though.

Two more times he lowers and lifts the weights. His head is sweaty, his hair wet. His shirt sticks to his body but I love it because it shows how hard he's working.

When he finishes, I help Brandon put the weights up and then he sits on the bench. For a minute I'm a little nervous because he's looking at the ground, breathing heavy and not talking. I'm about to ask him if he's okay when he looks up, pushes his dark hair off his forehead and smiles. "Damn that felt good."

There is the Brandon I know. The one who loved playing ball with me and who always carried one with him. The one he always was when it was just the two of us, when he played because he wanted to and not because he thought it's who he was.

I knew it wouldn't take long.

"See, you'll be out there messing people up on the field in no time." I shut my mouth, embarrassed by the sadness in my voice.

"Al." He touches my shoulder.

"Don't." I shake my head. "It's no different than it was before. You've always planned on being out there."

And I always planned on being here.

Chapter 14

Brandon

Hot water runs down my body, massaging what I know will be sore tomorrow. My bags are sitting on the floor in Alec's room. He's at the store picking up a few things and looking for a movie or something for us to watch tonight.

Ever since we left the gym I haven't stopped thinking about how it felt when I finished my workout. My body thrives off being active like that. It's always been something I love but then he said what he did about me being out on the field and I froze up.

Not just because of him—because I know the look that was on his face and heard the sadness blended with bitterness there—but because of me. Because as real as it feels, it's fake too. It's the road that leads to Brandon Chase number forty-three. Of a lifetime of being the other me.

After dipping my head under the spray one more time, I turn the water off and get out. A pair of clean shorts, boxer-briefs, and a T-shirt waits on the counter for me so after I dry off, I get dressed.

Dirty clothes in hand, I head back into Alec's room, and stop.

What the hell do I do with my dirty clothes? I know it sounds stupid but I'm really not sure. He has a basket in the corner. It's suddenly all I can see. His clothes basket that I'm not sure if I should use. It's crazy. I get that but it makes me realize I'm sharing an apartment with Alec.

Like a real couple would. We're going to watch a movie tonight and sleep in the same bed, and hopefully explore more of each other. It's what I always wanted. What I never thought I would have.

It's temporary.

Because of me.

Alec's words play back to me. How he wants to take advantage of this time. I toss my clothes into the basket and turn back for the living room. I'm halfway there when the front door opens and Alec comes in.

I grab the case of water out of his hand.

"Is there a vitamin or a health store around here? I should probably get some protein or something." I carry the water to the fridge and put it inside. Alec kicks the door closed with his foot and sets the bags on the counter.

"Yeah I think I know where one is. We can head there tomorrow if you want."

"Cool. I need help getting a little weight on." It's not that I'm small, but I'm smaller than I need to be.

"I figured you'd want lots of protein. I grabbed a shitload of eggs and cheese and stuff."

"Thanks. We'll run to the bank tomorrow and I'll grab some cash for you. I didn't know you were gonna get all that."

He shrugs. "Didn't really plan it but it was there. My fridge is empty. Makes sense."

We play two games of Madden and make it through a movie.

I haven't touched him the whole time and I'm thinking that's a really shitty way for us to be enjoying this summer together, so when the credits start rolling, I turn to him. "I really wanna kiss you again."

Fire blazes in Alec's blue eyes as he leans toward me. I find that spot on the back of his neck that I like to hold and pull him closer...closer. My lips are so fucking close to his and just as I'm about to claim him, a pounding comes from the door, making both of us jerk apart.

"Argh." I fall back against the couch, moving my junk around so it's not so obvious I have a hard-on.

"Alec, it's your favorite you-know-what!" Logan's voice sounds from the other side of the door making me groan again.

"His favorite what?" I ask.

"He's being an idiot. I'm pretty sure he means 'gay guy.'" Alec goes to the door and pulls it open.

"What's up, man?"

"Nothin'. I was out and figured I'd stop by to see what you're up to." Logan steps inside the apartment and his eyes land on me for the first time. "Oh. I see what you're doing." Still he walks over to the chair and falls into it. "Hey." He nods his head at me.

"Hey." I know I'm a bastard when it comes to him but I fucking hate the guy. Hate that he'll be here and he's been here and that he's touched Alec in a way I haven't. That he's touched him at all. I hate it as much as I hate the fact that anyone aside from Alec has had their hands on me too.

Logan waits until Alec sits on the couch, before he speaks. "Sorry, man. Didn't know you had company."

At first I don't pay much attention to his words, don't let them sink in because Alec is sitting a whole hell of a lot farther from me than he was a few minutes ago.

"It's cool. We're just hanging out," Alec replies to him.

It's those words that catch my attention and make me respond. "Plus, I'm staying here for the summer anyway, so I'll be around."

"Only for the summer." Logan repeats and I start to push to my feet, ready to kick his ass but Alec puts a hand on my leg.

"That's not cool." Alec looks at Logan while he's talking to him. I sit back down.

"I'm just giving him shit." He looks at me. "Seriously, I'm happy for you guys. Glad you're together now. I haven't even known Alec very long but I could tell how much he missed you."

Ouch. I can't tell if he did it on purpose or not. And to add to the shittiness, I can't even say we're really together. How can we be when Alec and I have both given this a time limit?

"Yeah, how about we don't do the sharing our feelings thing, ya think?" Alec turns the DVD player off and the TV flips on.

"Guess that means I'm not supposed to tell you about my date?" Logan teases. It should make me feel better that he's seeing someone but it doesn't. He's obviously into Alec. What reason will they have not to hook up when I'm gone?

Reaching over, I hold the back of Alec's neck. Nerves make my palm tingle but the need to touch Alec is stronger. I've never touched him in front of someone like this but Logan's gay. He knows about us. And *fuck* I just want to remind myself he's mine, even if it's only for a short time.

Alec turns his head a little, looking at me out of the corner of his eye. I see the shock there, and I brush my thumb through the hair at the nape of his neck, making him grin.

They talk about people I don't know and Logan moving to a new apartment. I try to get involved but really I'm looking at Alec sitting so close to me and feeling my hand on him in front of someone else.

It's not the same as the guys on my team but it's something.

Logan doesn't stay too long. Maybe forty-five minutes and then he's talking about some club he's going to and out the door.

It was forty-five minutes too long if you ask me.

"You touched me in front of someone." Alec steps forward.

"I want to touch you again now."

Alec pulls his T-shirt off. "So touch."

Instant fucking hard-on.

We both step toward each other. My mouth comes down on his. The kiss is rushed, urgent. Need pulses through me. I've spent years wanting my hands and mouth on him like they are now—wanting to feel his skin and know what it's like to be with him in a way I've fantasized about.

I've been with a couple girls, but it has nothing on the feel of Alec's body against mine.

"Bedroom." I mumble against his neck.

Alec pulls away. There's a light switch by the door and he hits it. I practically run the five feet to the TV to turn it off and then we're stumbling down the hall and laughing, in a rush to explore.

I want to explore all of him.

We get to the room and Alec's hands are pushing up my T-shirt. As soon as it's gone, I'm kissing him again. And it's perfect and right in a way nothing else has ever been. *This* is who I am and *this* is who I'm supposed to be with but it's not the Brandon anyone else knows. Not the one they want me to be or the one I know how to be.

It's suddenly not enough. I push my hand down the back of his shorts, making Alec moan into my mouth. I want to swallow every sound he makes. Find a way to make them keep falling out of his mouth because I'll starve without them.

I didn't even realize I was still backing him up until the bed stops us. He goes down and I'm right on top of him.

Then our mouths are fused again and his hands are all over my back before he's rolling and moving, until my head's on the pillows and he's on top of me.

My eyes fall closed as he kisses my neck, shoulder, before making a trail to the scar on my chest and kissing his way down that too.

"I can't believe they cut you open," he mumbles his lips on my scar again.

"Alec…"

"Finally. Finally have you here." His breath brushes across my chest before he kisses me there a third time.

"Wanna feel you. Can I?" It'll kill me if he says no, but I also realize this is a big fucking deal for us. As much as I hate it I know what went down with him and Logan and I don't want to push.

"Hell yessss…"

He hardly has the chance for a breath after that and I'm pushing him up. Alec's standing on his knees and I kneel in front of him, my hand shaking as I reach for his shorts.

"I know. Me too." He touches my hand showing me he gets it. Not that I would expect anything else from him.

It makes it easier for me to push under the waist of his shorts. My heart is pounding harder than it has during any workout. If it's going to fail on me, this is when it will happen.

But it doesn't and then my hands are pushing beneath his underwear too and I'm sliding them down his body. My eyes follow the trail of hair down and then his erection springs free.

"Holy shit," I whisper as I keep pushing his pants down. When I get to his knees I have no choice but to stop because he's on them.

My eyes don't want to pull away but I make them find Alec's face, and he's looking down, at my hands against his legs and his erection between us.

He looks up at me, fear in his eyes. The need surges inside me to do whatever I can to take it away, so he knows how much I love what I see.

That's when I touch him. Just a finger at first, running up the length of him. Alec hisses and I wrap my palm around him, hot and hard. My bodies screaming at me, finally, *finally*, I'm being true to what I want.

When my lips come down on his, this time the kiss is slower, my hand stroking Alec's length while my tongue does the same in his mouth.

Alec pulls his mouth slightly away from mine. "Damn it… I'm going to lose it. You have to stop. I'm seriously going to lose it and I wanna see you too."

Leaning in, I smile, kissing him one more time and proud as hell I'm making him feel like that.

Letting go of him, I get off the bed. Alec lies down and starts to pull his shorts and boxer-briefs all the way off, kicking out of them.

"You're watching and not moving." He reaches for me, but I step back.

"Shit. Sorry. Couldn't help it." And then I'm pushing my clothes down too, this voice inside yelling at me, *You're naked with another guy. It's wrong…* But then that other part shoves in. The one that's letting out that sigh of relief, *You're being who you are. This is Alec…*

"Brand, don't let me lose you. Holy shit you're sexy. Snap out of wherever your head's going right now."

Alec's voice breaks through my thoughts and I'm throwing my clothes to the floor as he eyes me.

"Come here." His voice is raspy and I can tell he notices, because he sort of flinches a little.

"I'm here," I say and then climb onto the bed, and over Alec.

"Oh shit." My body jerks when he wraps a hand around me, my orgasm already threatening me.

"You feel so good." His fist slides up and down.

"I'm gonna lose it too. You gotta stop. I want...I want us both to enjoy it."

He laughs. "I'm enjoying myself."

"I want to try something, baby. Do you...do you have any lube?"

"Yeah." I roll off him. Alec leans to his bedside table and opens the drawer. I can't help but study every part of his naked body. He's incredible.

"Here." He hands it to me and I squirt some in my hands, before tossing it aside.

"I saw this...that's embarrassing, to tell you where I saw it, but come here. Get on top of me."

Ignoring that I just admitted to watching gay porn, Alec does as I say, leaning on one of his arms, and looking down at me. I wrap one of my hands around Alec and one on me, coating both of us. "Get closer." I whisper. He does and I take us both in one of my hand, and stroke us together.

"God. Holy shit." He repeats over and over and then pumps his hips into my hand. I do the same and then start stroking my hand again, jerking us both off together.

It doesn't take long and until he tenses and I give into the orgasm I've been holding off since we first touched each other. We both let loose, Alec coming at the same time I do.

He falls on top of me and we're sweaty and breathing hard. For the first time in my life...I really feel like me.

Chapter 15

Alec

I lie in bed with Brandon like I have every day for the two weeks he's lived here. We're both naked like we usually are when we're in bed and I can already feel the difference in his body from only fourteen days of actively training.

I'm on my side, my hand on the scar on his chest, while his rests on my hip. I wish like hell we had time for his hand to go lower, to show me how good he's gotten at it but neither of us get off as quickly as we did those first times, and I have to be at the cabins soon. We might not have had sex yet but we've done enough practicing with our hands that it takes longer now.

"You don't want to go, do you?"

"I didn't know you were awake." I roll over and he follows me, leaning on his elbow and looking down at me. He doesn't reply and I know he's waiting for me to continue. "Being here with you makes everything feel more real. People don't know but we're still really doing it, ya know? Living it, even if it isn't for good. I think being around Dad is going to make me feel like more of a liar and a fraud than I did before. And if he says something…"

"Hey—"

I turn my head and Brandon grabs my face to try and make me look at him. I push his hand away but make eye contact anyway.

"You're not a fraud. You're not going to keep hiding. That's me. Hell, you could be out by now if it wasn't for me. Don't be like that."

On the bedside table, Brandon's phone vibrates.

"Go ahead and get it," I tell him rolling away.

"Alec."

"Get the phone. It's not a big deal."

He sighs before reaching over and grabbing it.

"What's up?" Brandon says.

"We're taking a boating trip with Dev's parents' boat, man. You need to get your ass to South Carolina." Whoever it is talks so loud, I can hear him.

"Hey, Theo," Brand replies as I listen to their conversation.

"Don't 'hey Theo' me. I know you and that means you're going to punk out. There's quite a few girls I heard talking about kissing your injury to make it better."

Theo laughs and Brand freezes beside me. It's nothing compared to how I tense. When I try to get up, he grabs me, holding me tightly. Even though I don't want to, I risk a glance at him and he shakes his head, like he's saying "don't go."

Still, I watch him slip right back into that number forty-three jersey. "Damn man, sounds like fun but I can't make it. I have some stuff going on here."

"You're always bitching out, Chase. Have some fun. When you get back to school, you're golden for whoever you want, you lucky bastard," he tells Brand.

I already have to deal with my dad today, this is the last thing I want to hear. This time when I move, Brandon lets me go. I don't go any farther than to sit on the edge of the bed, my leg bouncing up and down no matter how much I try to steady it.

Brandon laughs. "Whatever, man. Did you ever stop to think maybe I have something better here?"

He's saying it for me but I still can't make myself look at him right now.

"What? Who?" Theo asks.

It's not like he's going to tell him that. Still, I listen. "None of your business. I'm out though. Thanks for calling." Brandon hangs up before Theo can reply.

Brandon touches my back. "Alec—"

"I need to get a shower." His hand slides off when I get out of bed. I'm not under the spray any longer than a minute when the bathroom door opens, followed by the shower curtain and Brandon is stepping in behind me.

He backs me against the wall and I let him. Buries his face in my neck as my hands dig into his hips.

"I'm sorry. Fuck, I hate this. Why can't I play ball and have you too?"

"Who says you can't?" Any other day I probably wouldn't have said that but I'm already on edge because of working with my dad today.

Brandon stands straight but I don't let go of him. "All the guys who won't want to share the locker room with a queer. All the gay guys who wait until after their sports careers are over before they come out. People who get jumped walking down the street. People who think I'm wrong to love you."

My fingers dig into him tighter. My pulse jacks up a few notches. I've always loved him, and even though I've never doubted he feels the same, we've never said it. It was this unspoken rule. Like it would make things harder because we've both probably always known this wouldn't last.

"I don't even have a backup plan after football, Al. How fucked up is that? I'm getting a business degree but what would I do with it? I've never thought of anything for my life besides playing."

The part that pisses me off is no one else has either. His parents are great and I know they love him but they've never pushed Brandon to think he could do anything but play ball. When he found it, they clung to that and I get it. He's good at it, and it was the first thing in his life he ever connected to. But what else could he have excelled at? His dad is a fucking professor and I don't think he ever told him school is more important than ball.

"That's because no one ever made sure you knew you were bigger than football. And you are, Brand. It's why I love you."

The water from the shower mixes with our kiss. I run my hand though his wet hair and he thrusts his body against mine. When I try to adjust, my foot slips and I almost go down, but Brandon grabs me.

"I know I'm a good kisser but didn't think I'd knock you off your feet." He grins.

I can't help but do the same. "Fuck you."

Brandon leans close to my ear. "Soon…" My body tenses because yeah, I've thought about it. Hell yeah I want to but hearing him say it is a whole different story.

"Now stop distracting me. We need to clean up before we go help your dad." Brandon steps away.

"You're going?" He hates being around my dad. "It's a training day for you."

He shrugs. "Don't want you to deal with him alone."

* * *

The sun beats down on my bare back as I drop a load of wood where Brand and I are helping Dad build the new fence. It's off to the right of the lake, close to the office and house where Charlie's dad lives. They store a lot of the equipment in here but the wood's getting old and rotting out.

Sweat drips down my forehead, as Brandon looks up at me from where he's kneeling down beside me. I don't know how he's wearing a shirt out here—wish he didn't give a shit about the scar running down his chest.

"You have dirt on your face." He stands and reaches out, smiling, his hand moving close to my cheek.

"You wipe his ass for him too?" Dad laughs and Brandon drops his arm, his eyes wide as though he can't believe he almost did that.

"Was just going to point to it," Brandon mumbles as I wipe my face with the back of my hand.

Dad grunts. "How's the training going?"

Brandon pushes the shovel into the dirt, digging another hole for the posts. "Good. Alec helps a lot."

I know he's trying to stand up for me the best he can but I wish he wouldn't have said it.

Dad crosses his arms. "Yeah, he was pretty good in high school. Alec's problem is he loved it but he treated it like a game. Wasn't serious about it. He didn't have the determination to try and make it anything more."

It's because I thought I could hide easier staying here and working at the cabins. I thought I could marry Charlie and be happy.

In that way, I'm like Brandon only I realize now I can't hide it forever. I don't want to. Brandon might.

"Maybe that's because he doesn't need it to define him." Brand shrugs. "He's bigger than football."

The shovel drops out of my hand but Brandon doesn't flinch—doesn't look up from digging his hole. That rush he always gives me, takes over, pummeling through me in a way only Brandon brings out in me.

I want to tell him he's bigger than football too. I want him to believe it.

Dad's shoulders set as he looks down at Brandon. The wheels turning in his head, making my heart feel like it will burst.

So I laugh. "Nah, but thanks for the vote of confidence. Dad's right. I just didn't want to put out the energy."

This time it's Brandon who tenses. The shoveling stops and he looks over at me. There's a tic in his jaw that probably only I would notice.

"That's all right!" Dad's hand comes down on my shoulder. "You've always belonged in Lakeland Village anyway. One day this will be yours—yours and Charlie's but who knows if she'll even want a piece of it, being off in New York and all."

That's always been okay with me. I don't hate it here, but I don't love it anymore either.

As I'm about to reply, there's a giggle from the lake. Without looking I know who it is. Ever since Brandon and I got here this morning, a couple girls have been sitting by the dock in bikinis. They keep getting closer to us and every time I haul a load over, I feel their eyes on me.

"You guys have some attention." Dad gives me this playful shake like he wishes he were my age again.

How disgusted would he be if he knew they did nothing for me? That I'd rather kiss, and touch Brandon? That the hardness of his body does more for me than the softness of their curves ever could?

"This one's about ready for a post." Brandon pushes the shovel deep into the dirt, with more strength than he probably needs to.

I watch his muscles flex as he works, wanting nothing more than to get out of here—with him.

* * *

It's after four by the time we're almost finished. Dad drags Brandon off for a little while to help with something while I'm putting some last minute touches on the fence. I don't turn when I hear footsteps behind me, figuring it has to be them or Charlie and Nate.

"Hi."

My insides freeze at the female voice. It has to be one of the girls from earlier. I thought we'd been in the clear when they went inside.

"Hey." I don't look their way, just continue to hammer, hoping she'll leave.

"Are you from here? My cousin and I are renting one of the cabins."

I let out a breath and turn. She's blond, wearing a jean skirt and a short shirt. The other girl, who must be her cousin, is with her too but she hasn't said anything.

"Yeah, I'm local."

Her eyes skate up and down my body. "I'm Dee. This is my cousin Rachel. Her parents used to come here and they rented us the cabin to help Rach get over a break up."

"What the hell?" Rachel hits her arm.

"What? It's true." Then she looks at me again. "Obviously it's not helping and we don't really know what there is to do around here. I was thinking maybe you and your friend could show us around. I figure we came here to have some fun, and the best way is help from someone who knows where to find it."

I won't be any fun for you.

"Not me. Her." Rachel shakes her head. "I'm planning on getting back together with my boyfriend."

Dee smiles. "Okay, well then maybe *you* can show *me*."

I feel like a fist slammed into my gut—words that have no business threatening to come out, at the tip of my tongue. *I'm with Brandon. I don't want to go anywhere with anyone except him.*

Until he's gone...

"I wish I could help you out but my buddy and I have some stuff we need to take care of. We're heading out in a few minutes."

"Oh." Her nose crinkles like she's never been turned down before. She's beautiful. I'm sure she hasn't.

"Hey." My eyes flash behind Rachel and Dee at the sound of Brandon's voice.

"Are you guys enjoying your stay?" Dad asks, his voice all business but I know he's also hoping to find out if I'm making plans with them.

"We are. We were just asking..." Dee looks at me and I realize I didn't even tell her my name.

"Alec."

"We were asking Alec if he could show us around, but I guess he has plans with his friend tonight."

"Yeah, sorry about that." Brandon steps up beside me.

"You guys can't take a night off from training to show the ladies a good time?" Dad eyes me.

Heat radiates off Brand. He's tense beside me, partially because he doesn't know how to handle this, but I also think he's wishing Dad didn't mention training too. Throwing out that he's an Ohio football player is the easiest way to get a girl.

"We have an appointment. We're meeting with a trainer," he lies.

"Oh, bummer. Maybe some other time then?" Dee asks.

"Yeah, maybe. We'll be around." As soon as the words leave my mouth, I want them back. The last thing I want to do is lead her on.

Rachel and Dee say good-bye and hardly make it out of hearing distance when Dad turns on me. "You kids are a whole hell of a lot different than I was at your age. Football's important but there's no way we would have walked away from an opportunity like that. You're young. You should be having fun. What kind of man walks away from a woman like that?" He shakes his head, honestly not understanding me. But then he wouldn't.

"Brandon's training camp's coming up."

"And he can't work out without you? Christ, you two have been attached at the hip since he's been here." He turns to Brandon. "I get it with you. You'll be outta here in a few weeks but"—he looks at me—"you I don't get. Not many girls like them 'round here."

"I—" Anger burns through my chest.

"It's my fault. He knows I need to train. I don't have a car or anything so he's just trying to help me out." Brandon's mouth is tight as he speaks. One of his hands is fisted.

"Crazy kids." Dad shakes his head and walks toward the office.

"Let's go." I drop the shovel to the ground. It doesn't matter that we're not completely finished, I start walking to my truck anyway. My head's pounding so hard it hurts my eyes.

I need to get the fuck out of here before I explode.

Chapter 16

Brandon

Alec's silent the whole way home. I'm driving his truck for the first time because he automatically went to the passenger side when we left. Guess he doesn't like to drive when he's upset. I didn't know that about him. It's one of the few things I didn't know.

Guilt gnaws its way through me. If this had been years ago, I would have found a way for him to know it was okay for him to go. He could have faked it. It's not as if both of us don't know how by now. Then he could have come back to me. It would have saved him the fight with his dad that I know is tearing him up right now.

But the truth is, I'm selfish. The thought of him being with someone else, or having to pretend he's into some girl makes me want to put my fist through a wall. He shouldn't have to do that. I don't think I have it in me to have told him to go. The thought makes me sick and now he's beating himself up over what his dad thinks.

As soon as we get home, Alec slams the door before leaning

against the back of the small couch, making him face the hall-way. "I hate him, Brand."

"No you don't." It's true. Even if he wants to, he doesn't. It's his dad.

Alec looks toward the floor. "He's going to hate me when I tell him."

I walk over, and stand between his legs. Setting my finger under his chin, I tilt his head up. "He doesn't deserve you if he does. Not you. You're the best person I know."

Sighing, Alec grabs my waist. I step even closer, and he drops his forehead to my chest. "I'm going to miss this when you go. I'm going to miss you."

I wrap an arm around him. Thread my hand through the back of his hair and hold him to me. "Me too."

As we stand here nothing feels like it's enough. I want to give him everything. If he'd gone out with those girls, hell, if he was with Logan, he wouldn't be stuck here like we are every night. Home, or training, that's all we ever do. I want to take him out and show him a good time. I want him to feel like he doesn't have to hide because soon he won't and he'll be a whole hell of a lot happier than he is with me.

"Let's get ready. I want to take you out tonight."

Alec eases away from me. "Huh?" Shock highlights his expressions.

"I want to go out with you. Let's go get something to eat and have some fun. Even if we can't show we're a real couple, we can pretend."

Leaning forward, he presses his lips to mine. "Let's do it."

* * *

"How many?" the hostess at Dave & Buster's asks.

"Just two." I try not to let myself get stressed out over the question. Two guys can grab dinner together. There's nothing wrong with that. She seats us in a booth. Alec and I each sit on a different side of the table before she hands us both menus and disappears.

"You know I'm kicking your ass at whatever we play tonight, don't you?" I tease, making Alec laugh.

"Yeah, right. Who's helping who train here?"

"Who's already getting back into shape and will be able to take you any time now?"

He looks over at me, and raises his eyebrows telling me he's about to say something he knows will get to me. "You could take me now but that's just because I'd let ya."

Heat scorches through me. "Ah fuck," I hiss. "Don't say that unless you mean it." I'm not a virgin but it feels like it. I've been with two girls, one trying to make myself believe I wasn't into guys—that I wasn't into Alec—and the second trying to make myself forget about him. It makes me sound like a prick but it's true.

But I know he hasn't. He has way more honor than I did. He could never sink that low to be with someone when he didn't mean it.

"Soon." Alec picks up the menu but doesn't look at it. "But I'm going to want you too, though."

Warmth spreads across my skin, a mixture nerves and desire. It's not something we've ever talked about before and obviously I've never talked to anyone else about it either. The idea is intriguing and I wonder why I never saw myself on that end of it before.

"Yeah?" I'm not sure why I'm surprised.

His forehead wrinkles and then he rolls his eyes.

Scratching my neck, I look at him around my arm. "Never mind. No shit, right? That was stupid question."

We both laugh. I slide my leg forward, and lean it against his, just because I want to touch him. As I do the waitress comes back to the table. My instinct is to jerk my leg back but I keep it where I want it to be. She asks if we're ready to order and for some reason we both laugh again before I tell her we haven't even looked at the menu yet.

* * *

"I was too busy playing football, a *real* man's sport to practice much basketball." I flip the orange ball in my hand as we stand by the basketball game in the arcade.

"Are you trying to make excuses for when I kick your ass?" Alec comes right back at me.

"Hell no. I'll still beat you. I just want to make sure you know when you get taken down that it's from someone who hasn't shot a basketball in years." The arcade is loud around us. People walking and talking everywhere, with flashing lights and sounds from games. I hardly hear any of it as I talk to him.

"Quit stalling and put the damn tokens in so I can shut you up in the way that matters."

I shake my head, as I put the coins in and start the game. As soon as the bell goes off, Alec and I start shooting. My first shot bounces off the rim and his swishes right through. Fucker. Luckily I make my next and he misses. We keep shooting and I stop paying attention to him until the buzzer goes off and I glance at the score. 28–28.

"Again," Alec mumbles before pushing more tokens in. I lose myself in the game for the second time until the buzzer goes off. I glance at the score.

"Hell yeah. Told you I had this, man." Alec gloats. My chest gets tight. Holy shit, I love his smile.

"Don't think you're getting away without another game." I put more coins in, determined to beat him. And I do.

"Look who folded under pressure. Can't keep it going two games in a row, huh?"

"Anyone can play basketball. I'll beat your ass in air hockey." Alec heads over to the table and I follow right behind him. We play five games, and tie three of them. From there we play pool, shooting games, fighting games. We talk shit about who's winning but really I couldn't care less.

By the time we climb back in the truck all the shit from earlier is nothing but a distant memory. Tonight we were like everyone else.

As Alec drives home, I reach over and put my hand on his leg. "I haven't had that much fun in a long time."

"Me either," he says into the darkened truck.

"That's because you were with me. How could it not kick ass?"

Alec laughs. "Cocky."

It feels good to let loose like this. Just to be *me*, and be okay with who that is.

When we get home, Alec reaches for the switch to turn on the living room light but I stop him. I stumble a little, finding him in the dark but I lean forward with my mouth by his ear. "Wanna taste you. Can I?"

His breath hitches. "Like there's any possibility I'm saying no."

There's a nervous flutter in my stomach but I try to ignore it. I want to soak up everything I can in our time together. I want to experience it all with him while I have the chance.

"What are we waiting for?" Alec breaks me out of my thoughts and then we're stumbling toward the bedroom. Hunger and need battle the nerves as I close the door behind us. I'm already hard, ready to have him but wondering if I'll get to feel his mouth on me too.

Alec turns on the light, and for some reason, my eyes find the football he gave me all those years ago, that's now sitting on his dresser. Movement from the corner of my eye catches my attention. I turn to see Alec starting to take his clothes off.

He already has his shirt over his head when I say, "Wait."

I fumble with the button on his shorts, and then push down the zipper. It's like a rush of everything hits me when I push my hand below his boxer-briefs—excitement, desire, strength, truth, all of it, creating a perfect game, all of it working together so there's no way Alec and I don't win this game. Together.

"Holy shit that feels good. I still can't believe it's you touching me."

"It's me, baby. I can't believe I get to touch you too."

His body's hot, getting hotter by the second as I push his clothes down his legs. Alec steps out of them while I'm throwing my shirt to the floor.

He runs his finger along the edge of my boxer-briefs, which rest higher than my shorts. My hand finds its home in his hair at the back of his neck as I crush Alec's mouth beneath mine. I'm not gentle and he doesn't expect me to be, which just makes more fire rush through my veins.

Closer…closer I keep going toward him, pushing him as I go, even though it takes him farther away from the bed.

My hands are rough on him, my kiss hard too and then we're stumbling backward until Alec's back hits the wall.

It jars us apart for just a second before I take him again. Damn, I love kissing Alec. Love the stubble on his face and how it feels against my own.

But tonight, I need more.

My lips kiss their way down his body. Alec's hand grips my hair and I can't help but laugh against the ridges of muscles in his stomach. "Excited?" I tease. He tries to move but I pin him to the wall with my arm.

"About to fucking blow up."

I drop to my knees, nerves trying to battle their way in again.

"You're killing me. You look so hot down there."

Tilting my head up, I think the same thing about him. His blond hair hangs in his face, his sinewy muscles tight as mine feel.

"Brand...please. I need you."

I've never in my life been able to give Alec what he needs. I've walked away from him and hid who we are and not always treated him the way I should. I'll be damned if I deny him this.

I don't know what I'm doing. All I can think is to try and do what would feel good to me, as I take him into my mouth. A couple times I almost gag but keep going and eventually I find a rhythm.

"Brand...holy shit." Alec's hand tugs at my hair.

That makes me take him deeper before using my hand to stroke him at the same time. He feels how I imagined he would and tastes how I wanted him to, like man, all strength and hardness.

When he tenses and groans out his orgasm I smile, so fucking glad I get to see him like this. That I make him like this.

Before I move away, Alec drops down beside me before shoving me down to the floor. My whole body feels sensitive, eager and ready to feel him too.

Alec jerks my pants off and I'm scared as hell I'm going to lose it right now because of the anticipation.

Not able to even find it in myself to be embarrassed, I say, "I can't believe this is happening."

A moan and my body jerks as Alec's mouth lowers over my erection like I did to him.

It's incredible. He is. The carpet rubs against my back, a contrast to Alec and the feel of his tongue and the suction of his mouth.

After my release, Alec falls down next to me, both of us on our backs, breathing hard.

"That was awesome," breathlessly slips past his lips.

All I can do is smile at the way he plucked the words out of my head.

Chapter 17

Alec

Things have changed in the week since Brandon and I went out. I don't know what it is or if I'm just a nutcase and making shit up but he seems lighter and more like the Brandon I used to know. The one who always wanted to have fun and teased his brother like crazy and made me feel like maybe those thoughts in my head didn't mean there was something wrong with me after all. Not if someone like Brandon could feel the same about me.

Looking down the grassy field, I watch him, forty yards away looking determined as ever. I'm holding the stopwatch in my hand, nervous as though it's me who has my life riding on how fast I can run the forty-yard dash.

"Go!" I yell. Brandon takes off and I hit the button on the stopwatch and what feels like two seconds later, he runs past me. Holy shit, he's fast.

But I know it's not as fast as he was. "Four point six seven."

"Fuck!" Brandon yells, before bending over with his hands on his knees.

In a few steps, I'm standing by him. "That's not bad."

"I was three point nine eight before."

"Which is fast as hell. There's nothing wrong with just being fast."

"But it's not what I *was*." Brandon shakes his head as though I don't get it and maybe I don't. "I need to be back where I was, Al."

Because football is who he is, and if he's not as good as he was before, he's failing.

"You have three weeks before you go back for camp. You'll train there. You still have your senior year. You'll get it back."

Brandon looks up at me, a smile threatening to pull at his lip. He straightens, and then reaches out, and touches the side of my face. "Thanks. I know you're right. It's just…hard." He scans the area to make sure no one is around and then brushes my cheek with this thumb.

It's something that would have freaked him out before but I still wish he didn't have to look around first.

Brand doesn't wait for me as he makes his way to the truck. He's tense and I'm sure it's because he touched me outdoors the way no straight guy ever would have. Still he did it.

"You're sexy when you run," I tell him while we're driving, hoping it'll relax him.

"Yeah? I'll run as much as you want me to, then. You're always sexy."

Playfully, I push him. "Suck up. That's cheating."

Brandon laughs, the tension from touching me in public already gone. "I didn't know it was a competition."

"Do you know us? Everything we do is competition."

"True." My phone rings just as the word leaves his mouth. He picks up my cell and looks at it. "It's Charlie. Want me to get it?"

"Go for it." After stopping at a light, I make a right turn.

Brandon talks to Charlie for a few minutes before telling her to hold on. "They're bored and want to come over and barbecue or something."

It's so strange to hear him talk like that. Like we're a real couple and we're having people over to our place for dinner. Which in some ways, is happening but we also both know there will be no Alec and Brandon in three weeks, and there will probably be no Alec and Brandon in front of Charlie and Nate either. Even though they know about us but we've never so much as touched in front of them.

Nerves push their way in, making me wonder how careful we're going to have to be. Frustrated that in our apartment, the only place we've ever totally been *us* things will suddenly be different.

Shit, I guess I should remember in three weeks, it won't even be our apartment anymore. Just mine.

I find it in myself to push those thoughts away. "It's cool with me. We can run and grab some food real quick. I think we're out of charcoal." We grill at least five nights a week.

"No, I grabbed it yesterday."

At that my eyes flash to Brandon's and his do the same to me. "Fucking-A…"

"No shit," I reply.

He shrugs. "We work well together," he says before he puts the phone to his ear again and tells Charlie they can come over.

* * *

I'm standing at the grill after just putting the steaks on. The potatoes have been on for a while now so it's not much longer until dinner's done. Brandon's sitting on the couch, playing a video game with Charlie, and by the sound of it, she's getting frustrated because she can't figure it out and thinks Brand's going easy on her.

I wouldn't be surprised if he is. He's like that.

Leaning against the railing I watch them. The sliding glass door is almost all the way closed because it's hot as hell out here and we have the AC on inside.

Nate steps up to the door and comes out, closing it completely behind him.

"She's always been like that. Gets pissed if she thinks a guy's going easy on her because she's a girl." I smile. Charlie was out there playing football with us and kicking our asses at night games when we were kids.

I turn back to the grill, not really sure what else to say to Nate besides that.

"Yeah, but watch: just give her a few more minutes and she'll have it mastered and then she'll be giving my brother a run for his money."

I nod because that's true too.

"How's he doing?" Nate finally asks after a pause.

"How do you think he's doing?" It feels like a betrayal to talk about Brandon to his brother. What he tells me will always stay with only me.

"I think he's happier than I've seen him in a long-ass time. Maybe forever because I'm wondering how much of it was fake before. But I also don't think it'll last much longer. He'll lose himself again when he heads back to school. How can he not?"

I close my eyes, take a deep breath, and open them again before flipping the steaks. Nate isn't telling me anything I don't know but it still sucks hearing it.

"I wish he didn't love football so much. It's all he's ever wanted and he doesn't know how to keep it and be…gay."

It's only all he's ever wanted because he thinks that's all he's able to do.

Nate continues, "I wish he trusted me more."

"It's easy for people on the outside not to understand. I don't think anyone who hasn't experienced it really can get it. Do I know in my heart that there's nothing wrong with being gay? Hell yeah. Does that mean it's easy for me to open my mouth and say it to people? That I don't feel like in a way it's letting people down or that I just didn't try hard enough to be "right" or a million other things? No. It's like there's this war always going on inside me and from day to day I'm not sure which one will win—honesty or fear. When you hear about people sending their kids to fucking camps to 'learn to be normal,' having nothing to do with them, or people who believe with all their hearts that it's wrong to love who you do…It's hard not to let that in. And he's an athlete. That makes it worse. You know what it's like, man. You've been in the locker room and heard shit people say." I glance over at him before looking away, embarrassed I went off like that.

"I might not have experienced it but he knows I love him no matter what. We'll always be okay." He shrugs. "I want him to be happy."

Me too.

"No one can make the decision to change it but Brandon though." I wish I could tell him. Wish I could say that Brandon isn't who everyone thinks he is. That he might be confident on the field but inside he's always struggling.

"It'll help when he gets back with his team. Playing again will help."

For Brandon's sake, I wish Nate is right. Brandon will pretend he's okay but he won't be.

When I hear the slide of the door, I look over to see Brand peek his head out. "Quit trying to talk about me, little brother, or I'll kick your ass." He ruffles Nate's hair like he's a kid and Nate pushes away.

Ignoring him, Brandon comes over to me, putting a hand on my back and looking over my shoulder at the grill. "How's it coming?"

It takes me a second to reply because this is the first time Brandon has ever touched me in front of anyone except for that one time with Logan and considering Logan's gay and Brandon was trying to stake his claim, this is different.

"It's about done. Probably just a couple more minutes."

"I'll make the salad." He disappears into the apartment and Nate goes in behind him. All I can think about is how real this all is now…and how much losing it is going to hurt.

* * *

After we eat we decide to walk up to the basketball court not far from my apartment. It's something to do besides sitting around playing video games or watching a movie.

We play a game of two on two, Brandon and Charlie against Nate and I. It works well for guarding purposes. I catch Nate feeling Charlie up a few times and I'm not going to pretend I don't enjoy my hand on Brand or his on me.

No one would know the difference either.

"Don't miss," Brandon whispers in my ear as I'm dribbling the ball. I fake and try to go around him but he's still on me. I turn, trying to back my way to the basket as I dribble, Brandon right behind me. "Come on, baby. Show 'em how it's done and I'll give you a surprise tonight." His voice is so soft there's no way anyone could hear him but me. But I definitely do, dribbling the ball off my foot, and of course he grabs it, takes it out and then drives to the basket, scoring so him and Charlie win.

"You owe me!" I throw the ball at him, which Brandon catches easily, laughing the whole time.

Both Charlie and Nate look a little confused but neither of them asks. Brandon's still laughing as we start to walk back to the apartment.

It's not long until Nate reaches over and grabs Charlie's hand. Sometimes I wonder if people realize how lucky they are to be able to do things like that. It's easy to take for granted that it's not that simple for everyone. When I glance over at Brand he's looking at me. He shrugs and gives me this sad smile and I know he's thinking the same thing I am.

It doesn't take long for us to get back home. When we step inside, Nate turns to me. "I still can't believe you let him get that shot off."

"Hey, I seem to remember Charlie getting past you a time or two." Brandon wraps an arm around my neck and pulls me to him before kissing my forehead. "Plus, I cheat."

I fist my hand in the back of Brandon's shirt and he keeps his arm around me. It sucks but I can't help but wait for it. Wait for him to realize what he did and be embarrassed and push me away. For Nate or Charlie to make a comment and ruin it but none of that happens. Nate just keeps talking shit about the game and Charlie rolls her eyes talking about how ridiculous guys are with competition. Then it turns into all of us teasing her because she's the only woman here.

It's so normal yet makes my heart race too. Brand ends up rubbing the back of my neck. Automatically I find Nate and then Charlie's eyes to see if either of them are staring or paying attention but it's... normal. So normal I relax.

For the first time in my life, I know what it's like to be in a real relationship. To hang out with friends and not have to hide the person I love. We're Brandon and Alec being together like we've always wanted to be.

Later that night, Brandon and I are lying in bed. Even though I didn't make the shot, he still paid his dues since he cheated. I'm trying to catch my breath and thinking life can't get much better than Brandon going down on me.

"Al?" He wraps an arm around me.

"Can't talk. Dying."

His voice is serious when he continues, "It felt good, tonight. Just… *being*, ya know? I know we can't… *I* can't, around anyone else but it's my brother and Charlie… They already know, and I… I guess I wanted it to be like any other night. We have to hide from so many fucking people that I don't want pretend when we don't have to."

"I don't want to pretend either."

Ever.

Chapter 18

Brandon

"Only two more weeks until football camp. I bet you can't wait!" Mom sounds like she's going to burst in excitement on the other end of the phone. I've got a fist squeezing my chest.

"Yep. It's what I've been waiting for. Senior year."

"Oh, baby. I'm so happy to hear you say that. I feel like I'm getting my son back. I knew all you had to do was start training again. You belong on that football field, Brandon. I'm so proud of you."

It's never been a question if my parents loved me. Both Nate and I have always known that. They're a little sidetracked sometimes and in their own world but they would do anything for us.

And they've always been proud of Nate. Even when Dad didn't make it home for dinner sometimes or missed weekends with the family, he was always there if Nate got some award at school or something. Dad's smart and he loved that Nate was too.

They never tried to make me feel like shit because I wasn't as smart as Nate but it happened. I didn't have honor roll assemblies

for Dad to go to and I didn't get told how promising I was...
unless it had to do with football. The older I got and the better I
got, Dad started making it to my games too. It was the first time
I had something that made me special—something he wanted to
support and a reason to be proud of me.

There's the part of me who knows it's to support me. That they
love football because I love football but then that stupid fucking
voice pushes in that can't help but ask: What reason will they
have to be proud of me if I don't have ball?

Nate was good at baseball and smart in school. He got some
"promising young architecture" award his freshman year in college. And now, I don't need tutoring anymore and I do okay in
school but with football, I'm better than okay. I'm *good*, I'm promising and I have a future in it. I'm scared to death to lose that.

"I've always belonged on the field." I confirm what she said.

"You have. But you're doing okay, right? No problems?"

"None." I switch the phone to my other ear. "Alec trains with
me every day. I'm getting close to my time in the forty again and
lifting what I was. I'm back up to weight and everything."

"Good. Don't forget your checkup. The doctor just wants to
see you one more time before you head back. Maybe you could
come early and spend a day or so at home. Or stay here until you
head back to school."

That fist gets even tighter until it's a struggle to breathe. It's
close, so damn close to time to leave here. To go back to my life
and to leave Alec.

"I don't know. It's been good for me here. Plus Nate and I
are hanging out a lot too. It'll be hard when we're both back in
school."

Mom sighs. "Okay, maybe just a night then before your
appointment. Have you gotten your ticket yet?"

No, I was hoping the day wouldn't come. That I wouldn't have to tell Alec I have to leave for a few days—that I wouldn't have to lose time with him.

"No. I'll get it today."

"Okay. Listen, your baby brother is being awfully quiet, which means he's probably causing trouble. I better go, but I love you, Brandon. Your father and I are so proud of you and all you've accomplished. You have to make it past this one last thing and then your senior year and the draft."

"Thanks, Mom. I'll talk to you later."

My cell slips out of my hand and lands on the couch. I lean back and rub a hand over my face. Every time I close my eyes I see football, see being at school and with the guys and laughing when I feel like screaming.

It chokes me, the future I've set up for myself that most people would die for—that everyone thinks I love. Because why wouldn't I?

My muscles twitch, begging for me to let the pressure building inside me out the only way I know how.

Alec isn't here and I could always walk or run wherever I want to go but I head to the spare room instead. Because even though my body loves the feel of working it hard, I need him too. I want to be here when he gets back because Alec feels better than anything else.

It should make me feel weak and in some ways it does but strong too. I shake my head, not knowing what the hell I'm thinking, and just needing to be physical.

Alec doesn't have a lot in the room but there's a treadmill and weight bench and we put in a bar for pull-ups about two weeks ago.

After tossing my shirt to the floor, I head to the treadmill first.

For twenty minutes I run as fast as I can, as though the machine is going to help me outrun my life. When I'm here, I'm going and going trying to find a way to leave all the shit behind. It doesn't matter if I play ball or not when I'm working out and the only other place I feel like that is with Alec.

Sweat runs down my body, trying to wash it all away. Mom's pride and how easy it could be for me to lose it—by losing football.

My body is still tight, still trying to fight off that suffocating feeling that chases me down so often.

Lifting doesn't help either, despite the burn in my muscles, so I jump up, my hands gripping the bar and pull myself up, over and over again. My arms start to shake as I continue my pull-ups but when I'm in the zone like this, it's usually pretty easy to ignore.

My hands slip off the bar when something runs down the center of my back. Whipping around, I see Alec standing behind me with a big-ass smile on his face.

"You scared the shit out of me, man." I push him but Alec grabs my arm, laughing.

"You screamed like a little girl," he taunts, which is a lie, but it doesn't stop me from pulling him closer while sticking my foot out so he trips. Alec goes down but the bastard doesn't let go of me and I go with him and then we're both wrestling around on the floor, trying to get the best of each other.

He rolls over so he's on top but it doesn't last long. I don't go easy on him but then I don't have to. He almost matches me in height and muscles and it's hot as hell to be able to just let go with him because we're so evenly matched.

When I get on top of him again, he thrashes and I almost lose my grip but then I lower my head and press a kiss to his lips.

"Do you know how hot it is to walk in and see you like that? I didn't realize it but I have a thing for backs." Alec kisses me this time and then I roll off him.

"Don't say shit like that to me until after I get out of the shower. I'm sweating like crazy." After standing I head straight for the bathroom and take the fastest shower in the history of the world. My dick's hard, remembering the feel of him beneath me and hearing his words play over in my head.

I jump out of the shower, dry off and then wrap a towel around my waist. It's not until I head into the bedroom and see Alec sitting on the side of the bed that I realize I'm happy. Ten minutes ago I felt like I wanted to bust out of my skin but laughing with him and being with him wipes it all away.

"I talked to my mom today."

Alec sighs and looks over at me. "I figured something was up the way you were going at it in there."

The whole story pours out of my mouth and I feel like a pussy because it all sounds so...small. Like it's not a big deal. I just need to man up. Deal with it. But when Alec looks over at me I forget why I was upset or how I felt telling him the story.

"You're more than just football, Brand. You said I'm bigger than playing ball but when are you going to realize you are too?"

There it is—that feeling again that I'm invincible. That maybe he's right or at least it's a whole lot easier to pretend when he says it. I walk over and stand in front of him. "I feel like it when I'm with you. Like I matter for something other than what I do on the field. I was so pissed earlier, Al. So fucking pissed and I wanted to transform. To find a way to be someone else or like, if I worked out hard enough I would find a way to love who I am on the field instead of making people believe I do—"

"Brand..." He tries to stand but I step closer, my body not giving his enough room to move.

There's no thought, just words flowing from my mouth that I couldn't hold back if I wanted to. "I love you. So fucking much and I don't want to lose you. I know we said we'd walk away at the end of this but I don't know if I can do it. I don't *want* to do it... but I can't come out either. It's like the words are locked inside me and even I don't know how to find the key. I don't know how to be gay and play ball. I don't know how to be *that guy* in the locker room or even if they'll want me there if they know, and as shitty as it is, I don't know how to walk away either."

Alec puts a hand on my stomach, slides it to my side, and grips me tightly. His nails bite into my skin but I like the sting because it reminds me it's him giving it to me.

"I would go," Alec mumbles.

"I can't ask you to do that. It's not right. It's not fair to you."

He shakes his head, and I see the anger start to set into his features. "Fuck that, Brandon. You didn't ask, and if you did, so what? What do I have here? I go to a shitty community college that's a dime a dozen. My dad hates who I am. He makes me feel like shit and he doesn't even know the truth yet. I don't have a job, so what am I leaving? I can go to school there and find a job there. And I'll have you. Don't we deserve to have each other? Don't we deserve to have what we want like everyone else does? After everything we've been through, don't we deserve it more?"

Everything inside me is yelling, *begging* me to tell him yes. To take whatever he wants to offer me but I've been so selfish for so long when it comes to Alec. I can't do that to him anymore. "What would you be coming there to? To keep lying about who you are? To keep pretending to be my roommate and always trying to remember not to touch me? You're tired of hiding. You want to come out, and I can't be the one to keep holding you back."

This time, Alec stands, his body pushing mine out of the way to find room for his own. "Fuck you, Brandon. Do you think I'm not strong enough not to do it if I don't want to? That I'm so weak I'm going to let you hold me back?"

"Hey." When he looks away, I hook my finger under his chin and turn his head so he faces me again. "That's not what I mean. You're the strongest person I know."

Alec grabs the hand I have on his face, and lowers it…but doesn't let go. "Then trust that I know what I'm doing. That I'm not going to do something I don't want. This is what you need to realize, man. You don't see who you really are. You're worth it. Having you is worth the wait. One stupid fucking decision to go 4x4-ing one night and you could have died. Do we really wanna just give up when we know how easily everything can change? It might not be this month or next month but one day you'll be ready. I know it. I couldn't love you like I do if I didn't believe that."

He takes a deep breath. "But I won't beg you either. If you want me, Brand, you're going to have to decide right now because I won't let you walk away and then try and get me back later. We're in this together all the way or not at all."

His words become my knowledge. I don't doubt anything he says, and damned if I don't want to have him with me. We can make this work and one day it'll all be okay. We'll find a way to make it okay. One step at a time.

"I want you. Jesus, I've never wanted anything in my life the way I want you."

My mouth comes down hungrily on his. Alec opens right up for me and as my tongue finds its home between his lips, Alec's hands are pulling the towel off my waist. I lay him on the bed.

He moans into my mouth. It's sexy as hell and I want to

swallow every sound he makes. His hand goes to my erection as I fumble with his shorts. It's messy and frantic, not smooth and practiced the way I want to be with him but I manage to get his shorts down and he takes his shirt off and then we're moving against each other. I feel the hair on his legs brush mine and the ripples in his obliques against mine and it's so fucking perfect, the way we go together so right.

"Wanna be inside you," I whisper against his mouth. "I wanna make love to you, baby."

Alec drops his head to the side as I run my tongue up the muscle in the side of his neck. "About time."

I can't help but chuckle, and then I'm kissing him again. Scared I might lose control and ruin this before we're able to get started, I lean over and open the drawer on my side of the bed. "I got condoms. Wanted to be prepared."

And then Alec's grabbing the lube from his drawer. The rest is like a dream. I need to look at him so I push him onto his back. Pushing a pillow under his hips. Then, I'm rolling the condom on, then kissing every part of Alec I can while I prepare his body with my fingers.

He tenses a little, short breaths rushing past his lips.

"Shit. I'm sorry. Do you want me to stop?" Everything inside me wants this to be perfect.

"Rock steady up here. Keep going." And so I do, kissing and touching him the whole time.

Finally an eternity later, I know what it feels like to have every part of Alec. I'm inside him in a different way than how he's always inside of me. It's tight and oh so fucking right that I have to stay still because if I don't, it's going to be over.

"Holy shit, Brand," he pants, squeezing me. "Holy shit…"

"What's wrong?"

"Nothing…just…" And then he moves toward me and my body reacts by moving with his. It's everything I thought it would be, my body alive in ways I couldn't even imagine.

He looks up at me, this blissed-out expression on his face making me proud to give it to him. I want him to feel more.

"Brandon…" His eyes flutter closed but then he opens them again.

"Yeah…I'm right here. Holy shit, I'm so right here." I move faster, then wrap my fist around him and stroke as I move, needing to make sure he's feeling everything he can. Wanting him to get off on this too. The second Alec's orgasm hits him, I'm jumping over that ledge with him, as we both fall…and fall. Together. The way it's supposed to be.

* * *

It's been hours and we haven't left the bed except for getting cleaned up. We fell asleep but now we're both awake, the room almost dark as the sun sets outside.

My body has long sense recovered and I'm wishing like hell we could go again but instead I just hold on to him.

"Al?"

"Yeah." He's tracing my scar with his finger.

"I have to go to New York next week for a doctor's appointment. It's my last one before it's time to go to Ohio. I want you to go with me."

"Yeah. Of course. No problem. I think I can swing a plane ticket."

I won't insult him by telling him I'll buy it for him. Whatever we have to do, we'll figure out the money thing with him until we get to Ohio and he finds a job.

"The other day with Charlie and Nate here... When we didn't have to hide? I know I can't tell my team and we're not coming out yet but... I think I want to tell my parents. I mean, I *do*. They know you. I go home a lot... I don't wanna hide you there."

My stomach bottoms out even thinking about it—about actually saying the words out loud to someone. It was hard enough with Nate but the thought of staying away from Alec in my parents' home is worse.

He's quiet. Worry bubbles up inside me that he won't want me to tell.

"You used to tell me you were scared to tell them. That you already hated that they thought you weren't smart and you didn't want them to know anything else was wrong with you."

I wince at that. "Did I really say that?"

"We were kids, Brand."

That doesn't matter.

"There's nothing wrong with how I feel about you. Inside I know that."

He lets out a deep breath and I wonder if he'd been holding it.

"What will they say?"

He's thinking of his dad. I know it. "They're not like he is." This time it's me who breathes out deeply. "But I don't know. I think they'll be okay but... how do I know? It's not something any parent really wants to hear, is it?"

He shakes his head and again I wonder if he's going to say he wants it a secret from everyone. If he does, I know it would be for me, because he's worried about me. He planned on coming out himself, after all.

"Yeah... Let's do it. We'll do it together."

Chapter 19

Alec

We spend the next week making plans. Brandon calls his apartment complex in Ohio and asks about two-bedroom apartments. I give notice here even though I won't be leaving until September. We'll both go down for the beginning of camp but then I'll head back here to get last minute things taken care of before moving with him for school.

We spent time online looking up the colleges that are close to him that I can go to, and filing out job applications online. I think both of us want to keep busy so we don't have to really think about what we're doing and how it's crazy as hell.

But not doing it feels even crazier.

Brand keeps asking me what I'm going to tell my dad but I have no clue. It makes me feel like shit that I haven't told Brandon there's a little part of me that's relieved I don't have to come out to him yet. Who the hell knows how I'm going to explain to him why I'm moving to Ohio.

In between all of that he's working out even harder, sprinting a million times a day to lower his time in the forty.

"What time's your appointment tomorrow?" I ask him as we stand outside the airport waiting for his parents to pick us up.

"Eleven. We'll have to leave early to get into the city on time. Maybe I should have just grabbed us a room here for the night."

I look over at him, and he glances away. "It was your idea to tell them, not mine."

"It's not that." His eyes meet mine. "Okay, it's kind of that but it's not that I don't want to, Al. It's just scary as fuck. I'm doing it though. I have to."

I'm still amazed this is even happening and not sure what to think. We'll still have to hide but he wants his parents to know. That's huge for him. For us.

Before I can reply, a Mercedes pulls up to the curb in front of us. Brandon's mom, Judy, lowers the window and waves, smiling widely. I hate that the first question to pop into my head is, *Will she hate me after this?* I've seen Brandon's parents every summer since I was fifteen years old. They've always been cool to me and I know how much they love Charlie. They treat her like a daughter, but I'm her gay son's boyfriend. That's a different story. I'm the one who he's scared could cause him to lose his career, or the one who could make people treat him like shit. It's a lot to handle.

The trunk pops open. Brandon and I toss our stuff in before I open the back door. When I try to pull it closed behind me, I notice Brandon standing there like he plans to get into the back with me. I see the second he notices he's doing it when he gets this deer-in-the-headlights look.

He doesn't say anything, just lets go of the handle and then gets into the front.

"It's so good to see you, honey!" She leans over and kisses his cheek. "Look at you. You look like my son again." She beams at him, making me feel like shit for the urge to tell her she was always his kid. That she doesn't know him at all. That guilt doubles when she reaches behind her and squeezes my knee. "It's so nice of you to come home with Brandon. You boys have always been such good friends. It's so sad that you live so far away."

She pulls away as Brandon says, "Actually, Alec's moving to Ohio…"

She pauses at that. "That's a big move. What about school?"

I clear my throat. "I'm transferring. I've always wanted out of Virginia and since I'm just in community college, it's easy for me to make the switch."

Brandon cuts me off, "There's nothing wrong with community college."

I tighten my fists, wishing I could kick his ass. It pisses me off when he thinks he has to defend me, especially when it comes to his mom asking about school. Yeah, we're planning on telling them, but how many times are we going to have to cover when we do stupid stuff like that in front of other people?

"Thanks, *Mom*."

He looks up and catches my eye in the rearview mirror.

The rest of the ride to their house, Brandon and I are mostly quiet. Judy makes up for it with talk about Josh, Dad's work, her excitement over helping Nate and Charlie with their new apartment and how she thinks he'll probably ask her to marry him soon. "The good thing is they're both such smart kids. They both realize how important education is and they have a good head on their shoulders. They'll be smart enough not to do something now to jeopardize their future."

I lower myself in the seat. Will she think of me as jeopardizing Brandon's future?

As soon as we get to their house, Brandon and I take our things upstairs. I automatically head straight to the guest room and leave my bag there. I'm walking out when Brandon steps into the doorway. "It'll be hard tonight...I'll sneak in here though. They go to bed early so it shouldn't be a big deal."

But it is. We just got here and it's already a big fucking deal. Silently I berate myself for freaking out but I can't seem to stop it either.

"Maybe we shouldn't," I shrug. "Not till we tell them, at least. How bad would that suck if we got caught?"

He crosses his arms. "You didn't worry about that before."

Because I wasn't your boyfriend then. We weren't about to admit to them we're gay and I wasn't going to move into your apartment where we plan to lie to everyone, when one slip could easily screw everything up for you.

"It's different now."

Brandon flinches. "If you don't want to do this, tell me, now."

"Don't put words into my mouth. That's not what I said." What am I saying? I don't know why everything suddenly feels so screwed up.

"Brandon! Your dad's home with Josh. Come down. They're going to want to see you!" his mom calls up the stairs. Brandon shakes his head before turning his back to me and heading for the stairs. Trying to get used to faking it, I jog down behind him.

* * *

The night doesn't get any better after that. Brandon and I hardly talk. His dad asks about training and football, how proud they are of him and how excited he must be to get back into the groove of things with his team.

They tell him they're planning a trip to Ohio for one of his home games with a bunch of their friends. It's a big deal—his senior year and going to the NFL draft. My mind wanders the whole time. This is what I wanted—us to be honest, at least with someone but now I can't stop worrying what they'll think or if they'll be pissed that I could screw things up for Brand.

His dad reaches over the kitchen table where we're talking and squeezes Brandon's shoulder. "I have to admit, I didn't see this coming. You were always so different than your brother when you were a kid. I want you to know you've done well, Brandon. We couldn't be prouder of you."

I'm the only one at this table who knows what those words mean to him. To know what he hears in them. That he was nothing before football. His dad didn't see him doing anything with his life, and he has to make it work.

It takes everything inside me not to say something. Not to tell them how that makes him feel but then I see it, all smiles and love…they look at him differently than my dad looks at me. How can I hate them when they don't know what they're doing?

"I think I'm going to go to bed early. I haven't felt real well since we landed." I push to my feet.

"Oh no. You should have said something," Judy says.

"It's okay. I'm sure I'll feel better after some sleep." No matter how hard I try not to, I can't stop my eyes from finding Brandon's. His hands grip the table, like he wants to stand but doesn't know if he should. I give him a small shake of my head, which makes his eyebrows squeeze together.

He would come. If I wanted him to, he would make some excuse and follow me up.

"Thanks for having me. I'll see everyone in the morning."

Without another word, I make my way upstairs.

* * *

The room is pitch black and my eyes wide open when I hear the door. It clicks behind Brandon and seconds later he's crawling into bed with me.

"I'm sorry," I say the second he's next to me. I grab on to his hip and he puts a hand behind my neck.

"It's okay. Feels kind of good not to be the one who's freaking out this time."

We both laugh quietly. Brandon waits until I finally say, "I don't know what's wrong with me. I just keep thinking about what we're going to do. They could be like my dad, Brand. What the hell would I do if your parents came down on you because of *me*? All you want is to make them proud and what if I screw that up?"

He tightens his grip on my neck and pulls me toward him. "You won't. Not you, okay? You're the only thing that's completely real in my life. They're my parents. They'll understand. When they see how much you mean to me, they'll understand."

I squeeze him tighter too. "Okay."

But we both know there's no guarantee he's right.

* * *

The doctor runs all sorts of tests on Brandon. Stress tests where they make him run on a treadmill, EKG's...on and on and on. I'm sure the doctor wonders why I'm here with him but of course he doesn't ask. Brandon goes through everything he's supposed to and all the results come out great.

It's not often there are side effects after an injury like Brandon's, I guess, but with someone as active as he is, they want to continue with checkups every couple months.

We take the train back, feeling a lot less stressed then we did on the way in. Maybe that was part of my freak-out from last night. I was worried about him. Tonight has to be better.

We play games on our phone and I text Charlie a few times to tell her what's going on. It feels almost like it did when we were at my apartment...normal.

Brandon left his truck at the station and it doesn't take us long to drive back to his parents' house from there.

"So he really said everything is great?" she asks the second we walk in the door.

Brandon grins. "I'm pretty sure he said I was in incredible shape. Smart doctor." She swats his arm and we all laugh.

"Well Mr. Incredible Shape, I made lasagna for dinner because I know you love it. Maybe now I'll hold it hostage."

"You wouldn't dare." He wraps an arm around his mom before looking at me, "I'll hold her. You grab the food!" he teases and I can't help but just want to watch him. I've gotten used to seeing him like this again—that old Brandon from when we first met and I'm glad to have him back for good.

Judy ruffles his hair and Brandon lets go of her.

His dad comes home about an hour later and we sit at the table, his little brother in a highchair, and eat. His parents ask me about school and I tell them I'm going to be an engineer. We joke about how, when they came to Virginia all those years ago, they never expected that Nate would fall in love and Brandon would meet one of his best friends.

My eyes flash to Brandon at that, scared he's going to take that opportunity to tell them but he just winks at me, making me instantly relax.

After dinner his dad goes into the office for a little while and Brandon and I play with Josh. He climbs all over Brand who tickles him and teases him and tells him he's going to teach him to play football when he gets older.

Brandon hits my arm. "I taught him to play," he tells Josh.

"Fu—I mean, forget you. He likes people to think that but I'm really the one who schooled him. I mean, he was all right before we met but I taught him everything he knows," I tease back.

Josh looks at us like we're fucking idiots, which we probably are before he picks up a block. "Block. Build."

Brandon shakes his head, but smiles. "Figures. He's just like Nate."

We build one thing after another with Josh before their mom comes to get him for a bath. My stomach starts tying into knots as we wait.

"You sure?" I ask him.

"I'm doing this." Brandon stands up and shakes his hands out as though they fell sleep.

"Hey." I grab his wrist, hoping this isn't when they decide to come back downstairs. "We're going to be okay."

Quickly, Brandon leans forward and kisses my forehead. "I know."

I can't help but wonder if this is another thing like last night—where we say one thing but we're really thinking another.

A noise on the stairs makes us pull apart. "Do you boys want to watch a movie or play a game or something?" Brandon's mom steps into the living room.

Brandon takes a deep breath and I physically fight myself not to reach for him.

"Actually, Mom. I was wondering if I could talk to you and Dad for a few minutes. It's important."

Chapter 20

Brandon

I'm going to throw up. My brain keeps telling me it won't matter. My parents aren't the type who make homophobic slurs like Alec's dad. They've always been fairly liberal, saying everyone has the right to live how they want to.

But I think it's different when the "everyone" in question isn't their son. Who wants this for their children? And as much as I hate it, I can't stop thinking that I don't want to let them down. That I want them to be proud of whom I am. But loving Alec shouldn't change that. It doesn't mean it won't, though.

Still, I have to do this too. I have to do it for Alec. For me. For us.

Mom sort of cocks her head at me, her eyebrows crinkle, the look on her face saying she knows this is more than just important. I've never come to them and said I need to talk. It's always been easier to just pretend everything is okay. There's already too much lying in my life though and I need to be honest about who I am in as many places as I can.

"Sure, Brandon. Let me go get your father." She turns and heads for Dad's office. The second she's out of sight, I face Alec.

"Tell me we can do this, Al. Tell me we need to."

My hands are shaking so I shove them in my pockets, trying not to look any weaker than I've proven I am.

"We can do this."

At that I pull one shaky hand free, hold the back of his neck and press our foreheads together. "We got this," I whisper.

"We got it."

We pull away just as Mom and Dad round the corner from the side of the stairs and make their way into the living room.

Nodding my head toward the couch, I say, "You can sit down."

"Brandon, what's going on? You're scaring me. Did something happen at the doctor?" Mom's eyes are wide, frantic. Dad grabs a hold of her hand.

"No, it's not my health. I swear. Everything's okay there."

Mom nods and Dad sits, pulling her with him. My feet won't stop moving though, carrying me back and forth as I pace in front of them. They only stop when Alec grabs my wrist and nods toward the dark blue couch across from my parents before he walks over and sits.

Yeah. Sitting. That sounds good, so I go down beside him. My leg bounces up and down and all I can think is it did the same thing before I told Nate I'm gay. That was almost two years ago and I'm still losing my shit like this? That thought is what makes me lift my head to meet my parents' eyes. Fear and worry radiate off them and I can't help but think they have to be relieved when I tell them I love Alec. Things could be so much worse than that.

After pulling a deep breath in, I let it out before saying, "I'm kind of…gay."

Silence is all that meets me.

"I mean, just gay. Not kind of gay. I…" My words trail off when Alec reaches over and puts a hand on my leg. I still have no idea how they're going to reply but this weight drops off my shoulders, because I was man enough to get the words out. Because he's strong enough to stand by me.

"Gay? I don't understand, Brandon." Mom's eyes are already getting glassy.

Dad's are directly on me. "I think it's pretty self-explanatory, honey."

If this were any other conversation, I'd laugh at Dad's words. But it's not and this is important. I have to get the words out.

"I'm with Alec…I'm in love with him. I have been since we first went to The Village."

The tears are free now, rolling down Mom's face. Dad wraps an arm around her.

"I love him too." Alec's voice is quiet, yet strong.

"We've tried to walk away. Tried not to feel it but…it wouldn't go away. I can't fight it anymore. We wanna really be together now."

At that Mom turns, buries her face in Dad's shoulder, her own shaking up and down, soft cries hitting me. Dad shushes her, that urge to vomit crawling up my throat again. *I made her cry. They're disappointed. Disgusted. They're going to walk away from me or want me to walk away from Alec.*

"I would do anything for him. I don't want him to lose football. We're going to keep it quiet. No one else will know." There's desperation in Alec's voice now, trying to make things better for me. And as hard as this is, that gives me strength—that kind of loyalty.

Mom cries harder and Dad looks over her head at me, looking older than I've ever seen from him. When Alec's hand moves toward mine, I link our fingers together.

Together.

"I'm sorry, Mom. I didn't mean to hurt you. I'm sorry…"

Her head jerks off Dad's shoulder. "Don't. Don't you dare apologize to me for that, Brandon. I don't ever want you to apologize to me for who you are, do you hear me?"

I sit up straighter, the nausea weakening as Alec holds my hand tighter. "What?"

It's Dad who answers. "We're your parents, Brandon. I'm not going to pretend we're not shocked but we love you. You being gay doesn't change that."

Letting go of Alec's hand I bury my face in mine. *We love you. Being gay doesn't change that.* "It doesn't?" I can't help but ask.

Mom scrambles out of Dad's arms and before I know it she's kneeling on the floor in front of me. "No. Absolutely not. We will *always* love you. Always. Are we clear on that?"

I nod my head and then she's pulling me into her arms. I try like hell to fight it but can't stop the tears from falling from my eyes. Dad's arms wrap around us both, and we're all hugging and two words repeating over and over in my head. *Thank you, thank you, thank you.*

I have no idea how long we're all like that but when they finally let go of me, I turn to the couch to find Alec and he's gone. My eyes dart around the room, before landing on him, leaning against the wall by the entryway.

He looks over at me, all blond hair and blue eyes and smiles. Stepping around my parents, I can't stop myself from going to him. From pulling him to me. His hands tighten in my shirt and I cup the back of his head.

"Didn't want to intrude." His face is in my neck.

"Want you with me. All the time."

Before I embarrass myself by getting all weepy again, I pull away. Mom's wiping her eyes behind me. "I'm thinking we need to have a drink before we continue this conversation."

A laugh tumbles out of my mouth again. My mom doesn't say shit like that.

A couple minutes later, the four of us are at the kitchen table, rum and cokes in hand. Mom and Dad don't pull any punches; Dad starts the questioning. "Why didn't you ever tell us?"

How do you explain something like this to someone who's never experienced it? "I guess for a while I hoped it wasn't true."

Mom takes a drink at that.

"When I realized it was, I was scared and embarrassed. I know it sounds stupid but that's how it feels."

"It doesn't sound stupid, Brandon, but again, I want to be sure you understand that we love you no matter what, okay?" Mom sets her glass down and I nod. "I hate the thought of you holding this in. Does anyone else know? Was there anyone else before Alec?"

He shifts in his seat next to me.

"Nate and Charlie found out later on. And no...I mean, I knew before Alec but he's the only one."

Dad wrings his hands together. "And you boys have been... together for a long time?"

"Off and on, I guess. The first summer we met, we were just friends mostly but we both kind of knew, ya know? We kept talking all year and then the second summer, we really started to accept it."

"You've had girlfriends in that time, Brandon." Mom's voice cracks on my name.

"Not really. I made most of them up. I went out a few times just so the guys on the team would get off my back, but Alec knew and I didn't go out with anyone more than once. It got too hard and we broke it off—*I* broke it off my sophomore year. We didn't talk until Alec came to be with me after the accident."

I practically see the gears start to shift into place in both my parents. They know Alec came because I needed him. That he's the reason I suddenly started getting better that weekend. That he could do something for me that no one else could.

Mom downs the rest of her drink then sets her elbows on the table, her head in her hands. "You're my son. I should have known. I should have seen it. Known you were hurting. You've been in love with someone for years and I didn't know. A good mom would have known…"

"No! It's not your fault. No one knew. I kept it a secret. I made sure no one knew."

She frowns, shaking her head. "You shouldn't have dealt with it alone."

"He had me…I know it's not the same but we had each other." Alec doesn't look at either of them as he speaks. For the first time, my parents really look at him, study him in a way they never thought to do all these years.

"You're right," Mom finally says. "I'm glad he had you, Alec."

At that he looks up at them, "Thanks."

After that we make another drink and my parents ask more questions. We tell them about our plan to pretend to be roommates—that we're not telling anyone else, especially my team.

"You don't feel like you can tell them?" Dad asks.

"No. No way." He doesn't get what it's like. He's never been into sports. He hasn't been in the locker room and heard the shit people say. "Not yet. We wanted you guys to know but no one else."

Mom bites her bottom lip. "I think honesty is important here. I'm not going to pretend I'm not scared for you both. I don't know if you realize how hard it's going to be to pretend—"

"We've been doing it all summer," I interrupt. "And in a lot of ways, longer than that."

"The more time that passes, the harder it will be. It's not going to be easy on either of you. And I don't know if this is the right thing for me to say or not but I worry if people know, too. I don't ever want you to feel like you have to hide who you are. Either of you. But the world isn't always a kind place. You might have to make some very important decisions in the near future. Your dream has always been a career in football. The draft is less than a year away. What happens when you go to a team? How will you explain your 'roommate' moving with you? Is it going to be harder to come forward then, compared to now?"

A heavy silence fills the room, and an ache builds inside me. It's not something we haven't thought about but hearing someone else say it makes it more real.

Not sure what else to do, I shrug. "We have to try, Mom...I love him."

She tries to hide the fact that she's crying again, quickly wiping her eyes. "And we'll be here to support you whatever you decide."

"Thank you."

We all push to our feet after that. Dad hugs me. "I'm proud of you, Brandon. And I love you."

For the first time in my life, I've done something to make him proud besides ball. Funny how it's the one thing I hide from the world that does it.

Mom hugs me next. "No more secrets. We're a family and we deal with everything together. I love you."

"I love you too, Mom."

She surprises me by going to Alec next. "Your parents don't know?"

"No," he replies.

She pulls him into her arms. "If you want us to be with you when you tell them, we will, okay? My son loves you and you've been there for him when no one else was. That makes you family and we love you too."

Alec hangs on an extra second when Mom hugs him. "Thank you...thank you," he whispers.

When they part, I don't hesitate when I grab his hand. "We're going to head to bed. Maybe we can finish talking in the morning."

"Yeah...yeah sure." Mom stumbles over her words slightly. Dad looks embarrassed but neither of them says another word.

"Good night," I tell them, before walking up the stairs with Alec, the way I've always wished we were able to do.

Chapter 21

Alec

Brandon's upstairs with his mom when his dad finds me. My first thought is, *Shit, almost made it,* because we're leaving in just a little while. I don't know why I figured he would want to talk to me. How could he not? When your son comes to you and says he's gay and you never knew it, I think most guys would want to figure out what the hell is going on.

Brandon's dad is cool, but cool or not, I'm sure he's still trying to wrap his head around this.

After sitting on the couch beside me, he says, "This is even harder than the safe sex conversation I had with the boys when they were kids."

I try to laugh because it's pretty funny. My nerves make it too tough, as I wonder what he's going to say. If maybe they aren't as understanding as they let Brandon and I believe last night or what.

"Bad time for a joke, I guess." He fidgets.

"Eh. I appreciate the effort."

"I know we talked about this last night but I hope you boys realize how hard this is going to be." There's nothing in his voice except seriousness.

"No offense, sir, but we've been dealing with it most of our lives. Even before we met each other. We get that it's hard. At least this way, we can deal with it together."

"That doesn't mean it won't be a struggle, especially with Brandon playing football. I'm not trying to scare you or talk you out of it." He rubs a hand over his face. "I hate that my son has been carrying this around with him. That he was afraid to tell us but I feel like it's my responsibility to be honest. It'll be hard to hide how you feel and times when you're angry at each other that you have to do it. The football field isn't the only place Brandon's been known to rush."

His second attempt at a joke doesn't make me smile any more than the first one. "Rush? With all due respect, Brandon and I have been important to each other as long as Nate and Charlie have but you didn't tell them they rushed."

"You're right but until last night you and Brandon hadn't even been honest with your own families about who you are. You still need to talk to yours. You guys broke up almost two years ago and didn't talk until just recently and now you're moving in with each other and have this plan of being together, yet playing it off as something it's not. It's a huge step and I want you both to be ready."

I shrug because a part of me knows he's right. Still… "We love each other. We've denied ourselves for years. Don't we deserve to be happy? Just because some people don't understand, does that mean we shouldn't try and find a way to have each other?"

He shakes his head. "No, no it doesn't. And I'm proud of you both. We'll support you guys in whatever you do. You've been around for a long time, Alec. I'm glad two of my boys have found such good kids to love. I just want you prepared."

With that he pats me on the shoulder. I appreciate the hell out of what he said in some ways but I want to tell him he's wrong in others. We've already been denied too much. We've already hurt and suffered enough that we're due for a little easy happiness. I have to believe that. Screw anyone who doesn't feel the same.

"Thank you. I appreciate you telling me how you feel."

"We're here for you, son. Both of you, no matter what, okay?"

Even though I don't agree with everything he said, I'm thankful for him. For both Brandon's parents. Maybe this is a good sign. Maybe there's a way my dad will understand too.

* * *

"I thought your mom was taking us to the airport." I toss my bag in the cab of Brand's truck before turning around. When I do he's right in front of me, and stepping closer.

"I'm not ready to go home yet." He comes even closer until his body is aligned with mine.

"Can you not give me a boner when your mom could be looking out the window?"

Brandon laughs, pulling back. "Can you not mention hardons and my mom in the same sentence?"

"Deal." I grab the front of his shirt and pull him toward me even though I just wanted him to back away. "Let's not go home." It took him mentioning it but I feel the same. Right now everything is perfect and I want to hold on to that. Not only are we going to be together but his parents are okay with it. I want to revel in it.

"We're not."

"Where we going?"

"It's not too far from here. It's actually kind of like The Village except the cabins are a lot farther away from each other. I figured we should celebrate."

He raises his eyebrows. Looking at him, it's obvious how happy he is. "Celebrating is good."

Brandon sobers for a second. "People always looked at me and thought I had everything I wanted. Football, money, good family, girls but I was always fucking screaming inside, ya know? Now"—he shrugs—"I don't know how I feel about ball but I can't even let it bother me. I feel like I'm me for the first time. My parents know who I am and they're okay with it. And I have you. It's like I want to tell people *now* I have everything I could want. None of the bullshit was real before. It is now."

It's impossible not to let his words pump me up even higher than I'd been. He's right. We're right. And he just voiced exactly how I feel. "I'm really wishing you didn't have neighbors because I'm dying to touch you."

Brandon winks. "Then we need hurry our asses out there where there's no one to interrupt us."

When I push him, Brandon laughs. I'm doing the same as I climb into his truck. Brand goes to the other side and then we're on our way.

The two-hour drive is pretty quick. We head to the office where Brandon goes in for keys and then we drive farther out to our cabin. It's tiny, surrounded by trees. Brand parks off to the side and I see a ton of open space in the back.

"I'm paying you for half of this." It couldn't have been cheap to rent. Just looking at it from the outside I can tell it's a whole hell of a lot nicer than the cabins back home. But it also means I need to figure something out about cash soon because I'm running out of it.

"Cool." Brandon jumps out of the truck and I get out behind him. We grab our bags and then head up the stairs. He unlocks the door.

There's a fireplace, not that we'll need it, and a huge flat-screen TV on the wall, which we probably will need. The couch is black leather. There's a small kitchen and a couple doors off the living room, which I assume are to a bedroom and whatever else.

Neither of us move and I'm not sure why. "Feels kind of weird, huh?"

"Yeah." He slips a hand in my back pocket. "I swear I'm not trying to be romantic. I just want you alone."

I push him and Brandon stumbles and laughs, his hand sliding out of my pocket. As soon as he says it though, I feel a little lighter. His answer feels like *us*. Even looking at him turns me on and I love touching him but what Brand and I have always been about is just having fun. Sports, working out, talking shit to each other.

"Sappy bastard," I tease him before I drop my bag and grab his hips and pull him to me.

"I'd say I'm trying to score points so I can get into your pants but I've already been there."

"And I can't wait to get into yours tonight." Leaning forward, I go in like I'm going to kiss him, instead nipping his bottom lip with my teeth before walking away. "Let's go. We should explore or something."

Brandon groans. "Argh. You can't say something like that and expect me not to want you right now."

I only laugh as I head toward the sliding glass door in the back. We might not be out but times like this everything is perfect. If this is what we have to look forward to, there will be no complaints from me.

* * *

It's hot, the air wet. I took my shirt off a long time ago, letting it hang out of the back pocket of my cargo shorts. Brand has his in his fist as we make our way through the woods. He doesn't take it off when other people are around but he often has it off when it's just me.

"It's different here than back home," I tell him.

"I'm used to both of them so it all feels the same to me. We've come out here every once in a while since I was a kid." He wipes some sweat from his forehead.

"So you could have easily stayed closer to home and never come to Virginia."

Brand shrugs. "Guess it was meant to be. Nate and I were so pissed that first year. Actually, I'm pretty sure I told my parents we could just come here. We actually lived closer to here before we moved."

Nate had some trouble in school after the first summer we spent together. Nothing he did wrong. Like always it was Nate doing the right thing but when the right thing got star athletes from his school in trouble, people got pissed.

"What about the second summer? Did you ask to come here instead of Virginia then?" He looks at me and I wink.

"You know I didn't. Stop trying to fish for compliments." I hook my finger in one of the loops on his shorts before he continues. "I thought about it. I was scared as hell to see you again. It didn't stop me from wanting it though. Nate and my parents thought I was pissed because we had to leave home again. Really it had to do with seeing a guy again who made me feel shit no girl ever could." He stops walking and grabs ahold of the back of my neck. "And hell, I hadn't even kissed you yet."

"You didn't know what you were missing." I smirk.

"Cocky."

My body temperature rises even more when I think he's about to kiss me. Instead Brandon lets go. "Come on, baby. We're almost there."

This time it's me who's groaning, left hard and horny.

Brandon leads me to a small lake. There's no one around, just like he promised. Still neither of us wants our junk hanging free in the water so we swim in our boxer-briefs.

We're out there a few hours, screwing around in the water before we get dressed and hike our way back to the cabin. Brandon pulls out a football he must have grabbed at his house and we play ball for a while, tackling each other when neither of us needs to. It's only to feel his sweat-slicked skin on mine, and the weight of him—hard and muscular when he falls into me.

This particular time, I don't stop myself from threading my hand in his hair and pulling his face down to mine. Brandon's mouth opens up for me as I dip my tongue inside. Like always we go from zero to sixty in about two seconds flat and he's pushing against me, his erection rubbing mine.

No worries bog my mind down. No one's here to see us. We can do whatever we want. We're together and we're going to stay that way. His parents know and they support us. It's more than we've ever had.

I push my hand down the front of his pants as Brandon's lips move to my neck.

"Oh, fuck you feel good. How did I ever get by without having you?" He thrusts into my hand.

"You have me now."

My hand keeps stroking and Brandon keeps moving. Soon he's tensing and I feel wet warmth in my hand. Brandon rolls off me. We're both lying on our back, looking up at the blue sky.

"Holy shit, I didn't expect that. I can't believe you just jacked me off in the backyard."

At that, I can't help but laugh. I can't believe it either. "We're here. Might as well take advantage, right?"

Brandon rolls over, looks down at me, and smiles. "I guess it's my turn to take advantage of you."

* * *

After we get cleaned up, Brandon runs to a convenience store to grab something to grill for dinner.

There's a couple missed calls from my dad. Even though I don't want to, I call him back.

"Where you been? I've been trying to get ahold of you for days."

As though he can see me, I shrug. "It's been busy at work. What do you need?" Going to Ohio with Brandon is already a lot, so I didn't tell him about New York.

"It's been pretty crazy around here lately. We had some pipes blow in one of the cabins. We've gotten a little behind and I wanted to see if you could come out and help. It's been hard as hell without you here much this summer."

My stomach drops out. I've worked at The Village every summer my whole life. It's always been a second home to me and I know how busy it gets. He thinks I've been working all summer while I'm really just leaving him out to dry.

"Yeah, no problem. I think I have a few days off in a row. I'll call you after I check my schedule." *But I won't have much time before I go to Ohio for camp with Brandon.*

"Thanks. I need to run. Talk to you soon." Dad doesn't wait for me to say good-bye before he hangs up.

As he does, the door opens and Brandon comes in. "I just got some chicken and a salad. Is that cool? I don't want to fluctuate my weight too much before camp."

"No worries." I push off the couch wearing nothing except a pair of basketball shorts. Brandon hands me the bag with the meat before he goes to the kitchen and starts putting the salad stuff away.

"It's already marinated," he calls as I'm opening the slider.

"Cool. Sounds good."

We sit on the back deck and barbecue. They have a kick-ass grill off to the right side and on the other end, there's a hot tub.

We cook and then eat, finishing right as the sky starts to darken.

"Wanna get in the hot tub?" I ask Brandon.

"Sure."

He laughs before taking the top off. It's not long before we're both climbing in. It's dark out here with just the porch light and the little dots of silver in the sky. Brandon and I are sitting next to each other, one of the jets massaging my back.

Looking over, I see the raised skin of his scar running down his chest. With my finger, I trace it. "I forget sometimes. Then I look at it and I remember how close you came to dying. Besides the scar, you can't even tell, Brand. You got it all back, just in time for football."

"*We.* You helped. I was being a lazy, piece of shit. I hate that. It's not me."

No, it isn't. "You're you now."

Brandon moves in front of me, sort of floating in the water, with his hands on my sides. "I almost told them, Al. I don't know why I didn't. It should have been so fucking easy to tell my parents that I'm not sure about football. But…"

"You didn't want another strike against you. You just told them you're gay. You still think that's all you're good at. Or maybe it feels safe—a part of you who's still who they want you to be, even though you're gay."

He shakes his head, water beading down his dark brown hair. "No. I'm proud of loving you."

And I know he is in a lot of ways. Just like I realize it's still a strike against him too. The thought makes my stomach ache but then, I'm not doing anything to change it either. Brandon at least told his family.

"I love you too," I reply because it's easier then discussing the rest of it. That's what's important. We love each other, we're together and we're happy, which I really fucking am.

"Come here." Brandon pulls at me as he backs up. He sits on the seat on the other side of the hot tub. Now, I'm kneeling in front of him, his legs wrapped around me. "It feels good...that they know. I'm happy, baby. For the first time in my life, I'm really fucking happy."

I smile, before leaning forward and licking a drop of water off his shoulder. "I was just thinking that. I am too."

Brandon's hand massages at my neck, as I nip at the skin of his. "We're going to be able to do this every day. Finally."

He hisses when my teeth dig into him a little harder.

"Always."

Sliding my mouth up, I stop when I get to his ear. "I want you too. So much. Will you let me? Can I have you, Brand?"

Chapter 22

Brandon

I'm over lying to myself enough that I don't pretend the thought doesn't scare the shit out of me. That there's not a part of me who wishes we couldn't keep going with me doing Alec for a little while longer. Still...I'm intrigued by it too. I want to know Alec in a way that I've never known anyone else.

This will only be ours. Something he's never experienced with anyone else and something I haven't either. "Let's go." There's a slight tremble to my voice. If he notices it, Alec doesn't say a word.

We stand up and go about taking care of the hot tub as though we didn't just talk about what we did. I lock the door behind us when we go inside, wrapped in towels.

When we get to our room, I pull off my wet clothes and toss them into the bathroom before drying myself off. I hear Alec's clothes hit the floor and know he's doing the same.

"You brought everything?"

Determined to man up, I look him in the eyes and wink. "Obviously."

"We were going to your parents' house. How was I supposed to know?"

"A smart man is always prepared." Naked, I walk over to my bag on the floor, bend down and open it. When I find what I'm looking for, I stand, feeling the warmth of an equally naked Alec behind me.

He wraps his arms around me from behind, his hand slipping low. "I love that I get to see you like this now."

A breath hisses from between my teeth when he grabs me. "Shit…bed…"

He laughs and when he takes his hand away, I question how smart my words were.

I drop the condom and lube on the bed before lying down. Before I get the chance to do much of anything else, Alec's mouth replaces where his hand just was. "Fuck…" Going down on each other is definitely something we've mastered by now. I latch on to Alec's hair as he drives me crazy with his mouth and tongue.

My whole body goes tight in the best possible way. Heat, fire—hell, a fucking inferno burns through me from the inside out. Each time Alec moves, he adds fuel to it, kicking my need up another notch, threatening to burn me to the ground.

And right as I almost can't take it anymore, he pulls back. "What are you doing?"

He smiles but his eyes dart down, embarrassed. "I read it makes it harder for you if you have an orgasm first."

"You're killing me." Really, I like that it was important enough to him to want all the facts.

"I think you'll be okay." Alec laughs as he lies between my legs, his chest on mine.

"I think I'll be better than okay."

"I love watching you, so you're not the only one who missed out."

That's enough to pry my eyes open. I run my hand over his head, through his hair and down his back. "That's because you're cocky and you like to know you can make me lose control like that."

Alec smiles before leaning forward and touching his lips to mine. "Like you don't?"

"I do. I definitely fucking do."

My body freezes when his hand drifts down, past my cock and keeps going. Alec must feel it because he stops. "We don't have to. If you don't want we can—"

"No. I'm good. We're good. I want you."

"I won't rush. I'll go slow." And he does. Alec grabs the bottle of lubricant and opens it. When he touches me again, his fingers are wet. It's uncomfortable when he pushes in, and I know this is just the beginning. To distract myself I lean up, kiss his neck and his chest. Run my tongue over each cut of every muscle I can reach.

It's not long until I'm able to relax... and *feel*. This is Alec and he's everything to me. He stops to open the condom and put it on. My heart rate jacks up while I wait.

More wet on him and me and then he's holding himself over me, looking down.

"Grab a pillow. It'll help," I tell him.

Alec nods and pushes a pillow beneath me.

"Are you scared?" he asks.

"Shitless." It doesn't matter if it makes me look weak. I'm not lying to him over this.

"It'll be good. I'll make it good for you like you do with me."

Those words massage some of the tension from my body. And then he's there. I'm grabbing his sides and trying to relax as he's pushing forward. "Fuck…fuck, fuck, fuck," falls out of my mouth over and over.

"I'm trying." Alec teases and I can't help but smile.

Then he does. His eyes don't leave mine. Soon I'm moving with him and I'm tightening my grip for different reasons. I feel his quick breaths against my face and his hard body against mine and it's so fucking right that I wonder how anything ever felt good without him.

When Alec kisses me it makes everything that much better. His lips are gone and I'm about to complain but then he whispers, "Touch yourself."

So I begin to stroke and then everything is *really* better.

When we're done, we're lying together naked, too hot for the blankets. I know I said it earlier but the words still need to find their way from my mouth. "We could have had this. The whole time we could have had this." But we didn't because I was an ass.

"We have it now. That just means we have a lot of missed time to make up for." Alec's leg drapes over me, his chest partway on mine as I lie on my back. I find the spot on him I like to hold, the back of his neck where it meets his shoulders.

"Maybe later we can make up for more."

His lips press against my chest. "I love you, Brand."

"I love you too."

* * *

We've been home for a couple days now. Alec's been out to help his dad and even though I tell him I'll go, he tells me to stay and train. Ohio is just around the corner and I'm still sprinting like crazy, pushing as hard as I can to drop my time in the forty.

I'm a running back. I have to be able to run fast.

Plus, we have a tough conditioning coach. It's going to be brutal when I go back to school.

Alec's working up the courage to tell his dad he's moving to Ohio. I get it. His dad's probably going to wonder why the hell he's leaving school and transferring to be with me. I wish he would let me be there with him.

He wants to get his dad used to the idea of him moving before he comes out to him and even though there's a part of me wondering if he changed his mind about coming out with his family, I don't push. It's not something anyone can force someone else to do. It's personal, admitting whom you love and no one can do it in someone else's time. It has to belong to each of us.

I'm not going to pretend it doesn't stress me out though. I know he never planned on coming out right at this time but he was going to be soon. The fact that he's putting it off makes me scared he changed his mind.

It's not like I'm one to talk. Yeah my family knows but no one else. That's not something that's changing any time soon.

We're happy and Alec and I know the truth. That's what's important.

I'm at the park Alec showed me cooling down after a workout when my cell rings. Looking at the screen, I see it's Theo from my team. "What's up, man?"

"Chase! What the fuck's up, bro? You doing good? You ready to kick ass out there, man?"

He's the only guy on the team who doesn't drink or anything. The guy is as sober as they come but he's so hopped up all the time, you'd think he's on something.

"Hell yeah. You know it. Been busting my ass all summer. Got my releases and everything. Talked to coach. We're all good." Of course I need to do well at training. It's not like I'd get kicked off the team if I don't. It's something I need though. If I'm there I need to be as good as I've always been. Otherwise, what's the point?

"That's what I like to hear. When you getting into town?"

I tell him when my flight comes in and he does the same.

"We hanging out? It's time to tear shit up again."

Shaking my head, I lean against a tree. "Sure, I'm bringing my friend Alec with me. He'll be around when we're not at practice." The word "friend" tastes wrong on my tongue. He's so much more than that.

"That's the guy from your house, right?"

"Yeah."

"What the fuck, Chase? Why you taking him with you for training camp? He your boyfriend or something?" There's laughter in Theo's voice. Would it still be there if he knew the truth? That Alec really is my boyfriend and I'm his?

I don't let his words bother me. Alec's coming no matter what. "Fuck you, man. He's actually moving up there so he's going to be checking some shit out while we're there."

"Cool. Listen, I gotta go. Hit me up when you get into town, yeah?"

"You know it." We hang up and I smile. That was easy. It drives the point home that we're doing the right thing. We can handle this.

* * *

"Hey." I look up from my *Sports Illustrated* when Alec comes in the front door. "How was your day?"

"Good. You?" He drops his keys to the table and falls into

the chair across from me. Looking down I see the old New York keychain attached to his keys now.

"Okay. I think my times are getting better. I feel good. Talked to Theo today and told him you're coming to Ohio with me. It was cool."

Alec nods. "I suck. I still didn't have the balls to say anything."

"Hey." I nudge his foot with mine. "You're doing something a whole hell of a lot bigger than me. All I did was tell him a friend is coming with me. Don't give yourself shit."

"All I'm doing is telling my dad the same thing, Brand."

"So?" I shrug. "It's still different."

He taps me back with his foot. "Don't worry. I'm not stressing. I feel too good to let anything worry me right now."

"That's what I like to hear. I'm keeping my man happy."

Alec laughs and rolls his eyes. "Dumb-ass."

"Made you smile, didn't I?" I pick up his keys. "You saved it."

"You saved the ball."

I did. Looking at him, I wink. "You're using it though."

Alec pauses. "That's because I got the guy back that I gave the ball to. And now it's even better than before."

My chest swells as I look at him with what's probably a cheesy smile. When I came here, that's what I told him I wanted. To be the guy he gave that football to. To deserve it.

My body hardly twitches before Alec's getting up and running down the hall. I have no fucking clue how he knew I was going after him but he did. I hit the hallway just in time to see him round the corner into the bathroom. I'm right behind him. I have no idea how we get the door closed behind us and then we're on each other. He's wedged between me and the door, my mouth devouring his. We go from there to the shower. By the time we got out, the water's cold but we're hot enough for it not to matter.

Later, we're on the couch watching a movie when Alec says, "Hey, Brand?"

"Yeah."

"You wanna go with me to The Village tomorrow?"

I know exactly what he's asking. He wants me to be there when he tells his dad he's leaving. "There's nowhere I wouldn't go with you."

I hate that in a way, it's a lie. I'm still keeping him in the closet.

Chapter 23

Alec

We have half the floor pulled up in the empty cabin, trying to replace the hardwood that was ruined with the leak. Don't ask me why I thought this was the best time to tell Dad I'm leaving Virginia, changing colleges, and renting an apartment with Brandon. Even to my own ears it sounds crazy. Why would I travel states away with my male friend for no reason?

"I have an empty room that's just been sitting there. I figure it will be helpful to have someone there to split the bills with me. I'm gone because of football a lot so it's not like we'll be in each other's hair." Brandon lies smoothly. He now has an extra room because he requested to move. And it will still be empty when we get to Ohio.

"I want to explore a little bit. I want to be able to say I've experienced more than here, ya know? I think it's important for a man to be able to say he went out there to get what he wanted." In so many ways, those words are a means to an end. They're not me at all. In others, they couldn't be more honest. Brand and I are both fighting for what we want now—each other.

Dad's hand comes down on my shoulder. "I'm proud of you, son. I think that's a real grown-up decision. You know I left here after high school. Wouldn't have come back if I didn't have to." He laughs. "Hell, I thought you'd sit around here forever waiting for Charlie and The Village."

Hearing him, I realize he doesn't know a fucking thing about me. It doesn't matter though. I'm getting what I want and as shitty as it sounds, I can't help but smile because he's proud of me too. No matter what he's my dad and I want that.

"When do you guys head out?" Dad asks.

"Brandon has camp and I'm going to go with him. I'll scope out some possible jobs up there and get registered for school. After that I'll come here, finish getting things done and then go in September."

"How are you going to pay for the classes? You're all set up with your financial aid here."

"I'll fill it out any of the forms I need for school or financial aid there. Plus, I have some money saved since Brandon's been splitting the rent with me this summer." The lies are stacking up now. Brandon's parents offered to help me at first but I told them no. I've already decided if it's too late for everything to work out, I'll take a semester off.

He slaps me on the back. That's what he does. It's how he shows he's happy about something. "You're making some real good decisions, son." Then he looks at Brandon. "Maybe having you here this summer rubbed off on him—showed him what he could have."

The pride I felt with his approval deflates.

"More like the other way around. He's the one who helped me to get my shit together and start training again. Everything Alec does is all him, not me."

Brand looks over at me and doesn't turn away, as though he wants me to know he's serious. I give him a small nod.

"You need to tell your mother. She's gonna have a harder time but she'll come around. I'll have your back on this one. We'll make her understand."

"Yes, sir. I planned on it. I wanted to tell you first."

Dad lets go of me. "Do you think you guys can handle this on your own for a little while? I need to make a trip into town and pick up some more supplies." He runs a hand over his balding head.

"Yeah, sure. No problem."

Adrenaline pings around inside me like a pinball machine. I do my best to cover it up, not to smile or act any different until Dad leaves. Hell, I don't know why this is such a big deal to me. It's so small when compared to everything else but it's a step, almost feels like a sign. This is really meant to happen and we're really going to do it.

When I hear Dad's truck rumble and then tires on the gravel, I can't stop myself from turning to Brand.

"You look shocked," he says without moving toward me.

It takes a minute to sort through my thoughts. "It's really happening. I don't know why I didn't think it would. We're really doing it. Your parents know and they're okay with it. My dad doesn't know still." I shrug. "He thinks it's a good idea for me to go with you. I know it sounds stupid but I kept waiting for something to go wrong. It just...it feels like we've been through so much shit just because we love each other. Maybe...maybe it's really over. Maybe we paid our dues and now it's our time to be happy. Who knows, he might understand when I tell him everything."

It's a stretch. Knowing that doesn't stop me from clinging to it, from wanting to believe it because we do deserve it.

"You got all that from him not giving you shit for moving to Ohio, huh?" He grins, making me do the same.

"Asshole."

"I mean, I knew it all along. For weeks now, I've known it's finally our time."

"Keep talking shit and I'll kick your ass." One step, then another, I move through the cabin toward him. There's nothing around us except equipment. There's a sawhorse across from the hallway, some wood leaned against the wall.

We're alone and I almost feel like I'm high. It's a rush knowing we'll be together and knowing we're taking all the steps to make it permanent. It's not everything at once but it's more than we have and thrive off it. Off him.

"Holy shit you're going to start something I'm not going to want to stop, baby."

He's words reel me in, pull me forward instead of pushing me back. The way I feel right now, almost invincible, makes me know everything's going to work out.

"I don't wanna stop right now. I just want to celebrate and not give a shit about anything else."

At that, Brandon grabs me and pulls me to him. He backs up and I keep going, until we're partway down the hall. Then he turns, leans against the wall. I hold him there with my body. "I'm going to tell him. I wanted to anyway. We've been through enough, right?"

Not giving him the time to answer, I crush Brandon's mouth under mine. He lets me take the lead and I snatch it, dipping my tongue into his mouth to taste him. Holding on to his hips, I move against him. Kiss him deeper because this is all really fucking happening. I've been happy but the whole time, I've been waiting for something to screw up. Something to go wrong but maybe, *maybe* it won't.

Brandon matches me, every move against his body is one on mine. Every time my tongue retreats, he's invades my mouth. He goes straight to my head. We're going to be able to do this every day if we want and I can't wait.

"What the hell are you doing?"

I jerk away from Brandon at the sound of Dad's voice. I stumble over my feet and Brandon reaches out for me as I hit the wall.

"What the hell are you doing?" Dad says again, louder this time. His face is red and even from twenty feet away I see the vein pulsing in his forehead. See his hands in fists. I know I need to say something. Each time I open my mouth, nothing comes out. My heart is lodged in my throat. My stomach drops out and all I can think is I was so fucking wrong. He's going to hate me.

Brandon finds his tongue first. "I know it's a shock. I'm sorry we didn't tell you. We were scared but...I love him."

Even at Brandon's words I can't take my eyes off my dad. Can't make myself move.

"What did you do to him? Don't you fucking talk to me or my son. You made him a fucking queer! What the hell did you do to my son?"

That snaps me out of whatever trance I was in. "It's not his fault. It's who I am. It's who I've always been."

He turns on me, eyes narrow with hate. "You've always been a faggot? I didn't raise a faggot!"

"Hey. Watch your fucking mouth when you talk to him." Brandon steps forward but I grab his arm.

Dad voice is tight when he says, "Get your hands off him, Alec."

"Fuck you," Brandon spits out at him. "Come on, baby. Let's go. We'll get the hell out of here. You don't need him. He's not worth it."

"Don't you ever call my son that again! Don't let him touch you, Alec."

I'm frozen, my mind going a million miles an hour—telling me to make Dad understand. To walk away with Brand, and keep on going like we planned.

"Come on, Al. Let's go. We'll leave for Ohio early. Let's get out of here." Brandon's grip on me tightens.

That's when I see it—see everything fall into place in my dad's mind. He knows why we live together and why we're moving together. Why I wouldn't go out with those girls.

"You're disgusting. You think everyone isn't going to think that? It's wrong. What will your mother say? You're going to kill her. You think she wants a fag for a son any more than I do?" Seething, he eyes Brandon again. "You're a fucking ball-player. You think those guys are going to want to share a locker room with a fairy? What? You're going to go play house and think everyone else isn't going to be as disgusted with you as I am?"

Everything else is a blur. One sentence repeats over and over in my mind and it's the only thing willing to come out. I step forward, out of Brandon's reach. "It's not wrong. How can loving someone be wrong?"

I don't even see Dad's fist come at me until pain shoots through the side of my face and I fall to the ground. Brandon runs past me, tackling my dad into the sawhorse. They crash through the wood right before Brandon's fist connects with my dad's face.

Dad grabs him around the throat, squeezing with one hand and punches Brandon with the other. Somehow Brandon gets another swing out, again hitting his face and making my dad let go.

Finally I find my balls and jerk to my feet. "Stop!"

"Don't you ever fucking touch him again!" Brandon pushes off my dad who sits up, wiping blood from his mouth.

"Get the hell out of here. Both of you. I don't want a queer for a son."

I knew it. I expected it. That doesn't stop it from feeling like he just beat the hell out of me. Out of my heart. Brandon's parents still love him...Don't I deserve love from mine too? And what about Mom? Will I even get a chance to talk to her? "Dad."

"Get out of here!" he yells.

Brandon grabs my wrist. With a soft voice, he says, "Come on, Al. Let's go. We don't need him. We're good."

I'm not sure why but I pull my hand away from him and go outside. I climb into the passenger seat of my truck, Brand jumping behind the wheel. Rocks fly, kicking out from under the tires when he peels out of the driveway.

"He must have forgotten something...That must be why he came right back. Not that it matters."

Without a reply to that, Brandon pulls to the side of the road, not far from the cabins. "Fuck him, Alec. We don't need him. He doesn't know what the hell he's talking about, okay? He doesn't know shit. You said it yourself. We paid our dues. We're gonna go to Ohio and everything's going to be just like we said."

Ignoring his words, I reach out and rub my thumb over his swollen bottom lip. "He has a hell of a swing, doesn't he?"

Brand jerks his head away. "Don't do that. Don't pretend you're not upset." Then he cups my face with his hands, pulls me forward and presses his lips to my eye. I don't realize how much it throbs until he does it. "He doesn't know shit, baby. Okay? He doesn't. We're okay. We're gonna be okay."

Brandon doesn't sound as convinced as we both need him to be.

* * *

My brain keeps telling me it shouldn't be affecting me this way. I know Dad. I've always known what he's like. It's what made me scared of who I am when I was little and the main reason I lied about it for so long. I always thought I would be okay pretending to be straight and I could push it aside for the sake of my family.

The older I got I knew that wasn't true. I couldn't keep lying about myself and I didn't want to. It's just love, right? No one should have to be scared of who they are or be hated for it. That's what pushed me forward and what made the secrets get so fucking old.

There was never truly a doubt about how he would react. Not an honest one. Maybe wishful thinking and maybe that disguised itself well. I don't know. The only thing I do get right now is there's an ache inside me I didn't expect. Pain I can't see past and as much as I hate to admit it...a piece of myself buried so far down I can almost ignore it, who wants to pretend again so I don't have to be the person people hate on principle. So I don't have to hear again that whom I love is wrong.

Because regardless, he's my dad. I looked up to him. As a kid I wanted to be like him. It cracks me apart knowing he hates me.

That I know this is just the beginning. Even though Brandon's dad accepted us, he made sure I knew how hard it would be. I didn't realize it though. I might have thought I did but now I realize I didn't have a clue.

"Come on. Let's get you cleaned up." Brandon grabs a loop on my shorts, pulling me to the bathroom. He didn't touch me when we were outside and although it's always been like that—and I've never held him where people could see—it suddenly makes my jaw set.

When we get into the restroom, I lean against the counter, as Brandon wets a washcloth. When he goes to wipe my eye with it, I jerk my head back. "I can clean myself, you know."

"Never said you couldn't. Doesn't mean I don't want to do it for you."

My eyes drift closed at his reply, guilt tying me up. *This isn't his fault. I won't take it out on him.*

"Does he wear a ring? You have a little cut. Not bad and the blood's already dried up." Brandon wipes at my eye. Pain pulses through my temple but I ignore it.

"It's his wedding ring."

Brandon drops the washcloth on the counter. "I wanted to fucking kill him. I can't believe he hit you." He pushes my hair back and presses his lips to the side of my head.

"I don't need you to defend me."

I swear I feel the anger roll off Brandon before he pulls back. "You think I believe I need to protect you? I may want to take care of you but that's because I love you. I'd do the same for anyone I care about just like you would. Like you'd do for me."

"Shit. I'm sorry." I grab Brandon before he tries to walk away. "I didn't mean that. I don't know what the hell I'm saying." Still holding him with one hand, I turn to the sink. When I'm sure he's not going to walk away I let go long enough to wet another washcloth before I clean his lip. Without moving, Brandon lets me and then reaches in the shower and turns it on. Neither of us speak as we get undressed and get in. We don't touch either and it's hardly five minutes later before we're drying off.

It's early evening but that doesn't stop us from putting on shorts and T-shirts before hitting the lights and climbing into bed.

Lying on top of the blanket, I turn to my side. When Bran-

don's arm wraps around me, pulling me close, I forget for a minute that anyone can think this is wrong. It's comfort and love. It's
letting yourself feel free with the person who grounds you.

"I'm sorry," I tell him again.

"Shh." He scoots closer, squeezes me tighter, his arm wrapped
around me. "This is all that matters, okay? Fuck the world. We
don't need anyone else. Just this right here. Just us."

"Just us," I repeat. Hoping like hell it'll continue to be enough.

I take in a deep breath, really fighting to control what comes out of my mouth. "So he understands and I don't?"

"In some ways, yeah. He came out at eighteen, Brand. He told his parents and they kicked him out. He didn't have a job or anything and they just turned their backs on him. They didn't talk for years. Things are better now but…he gets it. He knows what it's like to be shut out from your own family. To be something that they despise more than…more than they love you."

And I don't because my parents accepted us. I both get it and am pissed about it at the same time. That doesn't make it easier to take though. Alec and I have always had that. When we were teenagers and no one in the whole fucking world knew who we were but each other. We didn't trust anyone with our secrets except each other. Now he leaves our bed to talk to Logan. Maybe it makes me a prick but that feels like he punched a hole through my chest.

"I should have told you but I didn't want to wake you up. It's nothing, okay? I love you."

Tugging my hand, Alec comes closer to me. Inside I want to kick my own ass for making him feel bad at a time like this. "Ignore me. I'm being stupid. You went through hell. If I'm not the one you need to talk to…" I let my words drop off there. As much as I want to continue, it sucks too much to admit.

"That's not what I meant. It's not that I needed to talk to him more than you. My head's just all screwed up."

Something freezes inside me at that. "Did you change your mind? Are you not sure about us?"

"No." Alec shakes his head before sliding his hand up my shirt and resting it on my stomach. Leaning forward, he drops his forehead to my shoulder. "You're the only thing I'm sure about."

* * *

The next day we stay home. A few times I ask Alec if he wants to go out and do something—anything, basketball, lunch but he says no. When he says I should go out and train, my answer is the same. "We're in this together," I say and he smiles, making me proud I'm the one who put it there.

We spent so much time apart before, separating at the end of every summer. If he had shit to deal with or I had shit to deal with it was the phone or nothing. And then I was an asshole and broke it off with him. There's no way I'll leave him again.

"Do you want to talk about it?" I ask when we're in bed later that night.

"There's not much to say, Brand. I know I'm being a downer. It just sucks."

I get it. The main reason I play football is because it's something that makes people proud of me. Because it makes my parents look at me with respect, like I'm good at something. I would have lost my shit if they walked away from me because of Alec. "I'll try to talk to him if you want me to. Or we can go together. Whatever you want to do..."

Alec rolls over and looks at me. "I don't wanna talk about him right now."

I hear it in his voice and my body already starts to react. "What do you want?"

"You..."

Pulling him closer, I let Alec have me.

* * *

"Come on. We're training today," Alec says when we wake up.

"Hell yeah." It's not even that I'm looking forward to working out as much as I am that Alec wants to go. It's a little thing but still shoots hope through me. For two days I felt like I was letting him down—like I couldn't be there for him. Him wanting to go out makes me feel like he's pulling through. We'll find a way to deal with this.

We get ready and head to the park. After warm-ups Alec says, "Let's check your times."

I'm stocky like I need to be, my muscles having come back quickly, but I need to be fast.

"Four point twelve!" Alec yells when I finish. "Hell yeah!"

"Are you shittin' me?" I ask. It's not 3.98 but it sure as hell isn't 4.67 either.

"No. You did it, man. You're pretty much there." Alec smiles and then moves forward as though he's going to hug me before he stops. "Shit. Sorry."

He's looking at me the same but something's different. Like I did something I don't know about. "It's cool."

But we both know it's not.

I run the forty two more times, my times all within tenths of a second from my 4.12. Afterward we go to the gym and lift for a while before heading home. We play a few video games. The later it gets, the more I think about the fact that we're leaving tomorrow for Ohio. Neither of us has mentioned it since everything with his dad.

"I think you'll like the apartment. There's a gym close too. Lots of people from school go."

"Yeah?" he replies before getting up and heading to the kitchen. "You want something to drink?"

"Just water."

Alec comes back with a bottle of water for both of us before sitting down by me again.

I try again. "We have time to figure it out but we need to start thinking about your stuff. I don't know if you want to ship it. I mean, we'll need stuff for the spare room so it looks like you stay in there. Or we can use your stuff. I don't care if we use yours or mine. Or we can get new stuff when we get out there."

Alec picks at the label on his bottle. I'm obviously not making him feel better like I wanted to. It's also obvious something's up. My gut is heavy. Still, I try to ignore it and say, "What is it, Al? You've never held shit back before so don't start now."

Alec sets his water down. He's never been the type to hold back. I have a feeling this isn't going to be any different.

"I just…" He looks me in the eye. "I can't go with you to Ohio right now, Brand."

Chapter 25

Alec

My mind is at war, with one side telling me to take the words back and the other who knows they're for the best. It's what I have to do.

Brandon doesn't reply. He only sits there looking at me, dissecting me with his eyes, trying to make sense of it. But how can he? This isn't something he's ever experienced. Hell, I'm struggling to work through it and he has so much on his mind with football and training. The way he studies me, the set of his body and the way he's rubbing his hands together makes me want to take the words back for him.

Hurting him has never been an option for me. Not Brand. He was all I ever really had. When I didn't understand how I felt or thought there was something wrong with me for it, he was the only person who knew. We always sort of took turns being there for each other and bringing the other back to the surface when one of us felt like we were drowning. When our thoughts or desires threatened to swallow us whole. I did it for him and he did it for me. He always felt like no one except me really knew him but he doesn't see that it's the same for me. I was lost too.

Only now my dad knows and he hates that person. I'm not sure how to deal with it. I thought it would be easy—thought knowing would make it easier but it doesn't.

Then I have my mom in the background there too. I've lost Dad but maybe there's a way Mom will make it okay. Or at least I can say good-bye.

"I'm not saying I'm not moving. I *am*. I still wanna be with you, it's just—"

"Don't do this, Al. Not when we're finally going to be together. Don't fuck it up."

White-hot anger shoots through me. "Don't fuck it up? I'm sorry if the fact that I'm dealing with shit, screws things up for you."

I start pushing to my feet when he says, "That's not what I meant and you know it."

He's right, so I lower myself back to the couch again.

Brandon slides his knees to the floor, kneeling in front of me. "We're finally going to have what we want. We're gonna be together."

But do we really have what we want? We're still hiding. Still lying. *But I'll have him.*

Brandon grips the back of my neck. "I fucking hate your dad for how he treated you and I'm so sorry for what you're going through but…it'll be for nothing, right? If we walk away it'll all be for nothing."

"I'm not bailing on us, Brand. You know me better than that. Hell, I just…" Brandon's hand slides off me, both of them resting on my thighs. "It's too soon. My head's all screwed up right now. I don't want to put up an act, pretending things aren't what they are. Listening to all your friends, and acting like I'm nothing more to you than they are. Not with where my head's at right now."

He shrugs. "Then I'll stay too."

I grab Brandon's arm when he tries to stand. "You can't stay. You have training camp. It's not like you can decide to skip out."

His jaw tightens, knowing I'm right. "I want to be here for you. You're mine. I *should* be here with you. Any time I've ever needed you, you're always there."

There's something sexy as hell about him saying I'm his, about knowing he's mine too. No matter what we've been through, I love him. "It's not like before, Brand. You're not ditching me. I'm not leaving you either. I just...there's shit I need to figure out. I mean, maybe I can fix it. Maybe I can salvage something with my family. I can't just give up without trying. It sounds stupid but I thought it would be easier. I didn't think it would bother me so much because I know him. He's still my dad though, ya know?"

He shakes his head, looking down. "It feels wrong. It's my fault and then I'm supposed to go and play football?"

"It's always been your plan." No matter what's happened, he's always just gone and played ball. He hasn't decided he wants to change that. Even though he's offering, he'd hate staying here when he's supposed to be there. Brandon's never given as much of himself to anything as he has football. I've always known that.

When the little stab of jealousy pierces me, I lean forward and kiss him, trying to wipe it away. It's not his fault his parents were okay with it and dad isn't. Not his fault that no matter what, he'll be okay. I want that for him. Hell for both of us. Like he said, we'll be okay. We have to be.

"You'll be busy anyway. It'll give me more time to take care of shit here."

"And then there's saying good-bye and the welcome back. We

can take advantage of those." He gives me a forced smile. I hate seeing it on him. Hate being the one to put it there.

So I try to wipe it away. I take his mouth again—hungry, needy, urgent. Brandon gives it right back to me and then we're in the bedroom. It's not long before we're naked and he's making me feel like only Brandon can. By the sounds pulling from his throat and the way his body shudders, I'm doing the same for him.

We're wrapped in each other for what feels like hours before he says, "It doesn't feel like we're going to see each other again so soon. Think it's because things are so different now with us? Because we're really together in a way we weren't before?"

Something squeezes around my chest. I don't know why I'm surprised. We're usually on the same wavelength like that. Every summer we used to say good-bye yet this one makes me feel more alone than the others.

"I love you."

Squeezing me, Brandon replies, "Love you too."

* * *

Brand stands by the door with his bags in his hand. We've been tiptoeing around each other all day. My body is weighted down. Like someone injected concrete inside me.

But somehow I'm empty too.

"You can still go."

The urge to say yes is there but I can't. I know if I do, things between us will get even more screwed up. "I can't, Brand. I have to figure this stuff out."

He nods. "I know." After dropping his bags he steps toward me. "I'm gonna miss you."

Wrapping my arms around him, I say, "I'll miss you too."

Chapter 26

Brandon

"Holy fuck, Chase. You kicked ass out there today. What the hell have you been doing this summer?"

I shrug, before falling down to the locker room bench. It's my first day back. I have to admit it felt good as hell to be out there. To run hard, and show the guys I'm still the player I used to be. That I can be better.

I fought like hell to be back out here and I'm doing it.

Fought like hell with Alec.

And as great as this is, it doesn't feel as good as him.

"Training. I told you that."

"I have to admit, bro." Theo sits beside me. "We were worried. You looked like shit when we saw you. I thought you were going to puss out."

I shove him. "Fuck you. Not going to let shit hold me back."

Theo and the other guys around us laugh.

"What's up with your friend? He coming out with us tonight?" Dev asks.

I rub a hand over my face. It's crazy but it's like I'm scared it's going to show on my face. One look when we're talking about Alec and they'll know about us. "Nah, he didn't come with me." Then, just because I need to hear it, I add, "He's still moving here though. He just had some shit to take care of."

"There's that new club in town. Wanna hit that up?" Theo asks. "Lexi's friend was asking about you."

At that I push to my feet. "Yes" is right there on my tongue. I've gone out with them a lot, pretending I'm looking for girls like them. Damned if it doesn't feel old now though. I'm tired of that shit and…it doesn't feel right. They might not know it's Alec I'm with but I want to be as true to him as I can.

"Not interested. I'm with someone now. Met 'em back home."

"Holy fucking shit. It's about damn time Chase's got a girl." Theo laughs.

It's not a girl. It's Alec. I could never want anyone else the way I want him.

"She's not here though, is she?" Donny adds and a couple of the other guys laugh, and they all bump knuckles.

"Nah, man. It's serious."

"She pregnant?" Theo teases.

"No dumb-ass. It's for real though." Grabbing a towel, I wipe the sweat from the back of my neck. "I'm talkin' forever here."

A burst of pride swells inside me. A year ago, hell two months ago I never would have said that. I would have played it off like I had plans or whatever excuse I could find. I'm done with that though. It's time to be as real as I can when it comes to Alec. That's the kind of guy I want to be. Brandon. The Brandon I am with him.

"Forty-three! Get your ass back here!" Coach yells from the office.

"I swear he's fucking psychic." Dev laughs. "Bet he's going to remind you ball is more important than women." Everyone laughs, that pride I just felt bursting.

Here, I'm forty-three, or Chase. Not Brandon. And I'm still lying to everyone about who Alec is.

* * *

I'm staying in my old apartment. Alec and I are supposed to move into the two-bedroom when he comes.

The guys on the team all tried to get me to go out with them again. I've gotten four texts calling me pussy whipped. I make myself ignore them.

It's not like I couldn't go. We do have a good time when we go out. They seem like assholes half the time but they're my friends. My teammates.

I just don't wanna be with them tonight.

I hit mute on the TV, watching ESPN with no sound. Flipping my cell phone over and over in my hand, I lean back on the small couch. Even though I've been working out all summer, my body is wrecked. It's not the same training on your own and being on the field. It's only nine and I'm already ready to pass out.

My finger hovers over the button before I finally push it to call Alec.

He answers on the second ring. "Hey."

"Hey. What's up?"

"Cooking some steak on the grill. You?"

I laugh. "You and that fucking barbecue."

"Real men grill, Brand." He chuckles, letting free some of the tension I didn't realize had taken up residence in my muscles.

"I wish I was there. That sounds good. I was too tired to eat."

His voice sobers when he asks, "Hard day? You're okay?"

"I'm good. I mean, it was a hard practice but nothing I couldn't handle. It felt great. Coach called for me afterward and I thought he was going to give me shit. He told me how good I did though. It kind of fell into place easier than I thought it would. We're starting two-a-days next." Two practices a day are hell.

Alec's quiet for minute. "I'm not surprised. I've always told you, you could do anything."

And he has. I also know he means more than football too. Instead of replying, I give him the only honesty I can. "I miss you."

"Miss you too."

"The guys wanted me to go out with them tonight. I told them I couldn't...that I was with someone now."

There's a cluttering sound and then I hear Alec curse in the background. "Sorry. I dropped the phone." I hear a smile in his voice when he asks, "You told them about me?"

The tension is right back only it's multiplied now. My gut is heavy. "I mean...not *who* you are but I told them I'm with someone. That it's serious and I wanna be with you forever."

"Not me."

"What?"

He sighs. "You didn't tell them you want to be with me forever. You let them believe you're with some girl you want to be with forever."

I push up so I'm in a sitting position on the couch. "I'm trying here, Al. What do you want? You knew I wasn't ready. You said it was okay. You're the one who said you wanted to come here and that we'd make it work."

The lid on his grill creaks. I'd meant to fix that before I left.

"I know...You're right. I'm having a shitty day."

My pulse runs as though it's trying to outrun something. "What happened? Is it your dad? Did you talk to them?"

"No, not yet. I'm going to soon though. I don't know why I'm being a prick."

The rapid beat evens out slightly. "You're not. You're dealing with heavy stuff. I should be there."

"You're where you're supposed to be. Listen, I'm burning my food. I better go, okay?"

Nausea burns through me. *No, tell him no.* It's like there's more than space between us, this wall that keeps building higher.

"I'm okay, Brand. It's just a long day. I started packing up some stuff for the move today. It's not you, okay?"

Alec has never lied to me. It's not him. But this time he did. It's me. If it wasn't, he wouldn't be getting off the phone with me.

Chapter 27

Alec

Mom hasn't called me once. That's the thing that makes it hard for me to pick up the phone and call her. Dad is an asshole and, in some ways, I know he thinks of her as second best in his life. Still she's a strong woman. She's doesn't let him run her life and he doesn't try. Mom has always made her own decisions. And even though she's never said anything against Dad's bigotry, she never makes the kind of comments he does either. She doesn't talk about fags and she never goes off about how they shouldn't have the right to marry and stuff like that.

I've never really known how she feels because she never told anyone about it. Mom's always been the type to just kind of mind her own business and be there for her family.

When Dad found out and said it would kill her that was one of the things that stabbed me the deepest. I've always had hope she'd accept me as gay because she is never vocal about that kind of thing. He knows her though. If he said it would kill her, I believe it will.

And she hasn't called. There's no doubt in my mind he told her and she hasn't come to me.

That's all the answer I really need. Still, I have to fucking know or I'm going to drive myself insane.

I'm sitting on a picnic table where I'd texted her to meet me. I look at my phone. I'm thirty minutes early and I don't even know if she's coming or not. Charlie asked her to meet me and all she told her is, "I'll try."

My cell rings and even though I don't feel like talking, I pick it up.

"Hey you," Charlie whispers.

My heart cuts off. "She's not coming?"

"I don't know. She left and asked me if I could watch the office. She didn't tell me where she was going and I didn't ask. I assume she's going to meet you. I thought you could use someone to talk to while you wait."

I laugh but it's one that I have to force out. There's no truth in it. "How'd you know I'd get here early?"

"You've been my best friend for my whole life, Alec. I know you."

"You didn't know I was gay." I feel like a prick the seconds the words come out.

"Stop trying to fight with me. I'm too sad to participate. I wish you would've gone with Brandon. It might have helped to get away. You guys need each other right now."

This is the main reason I haven't talked to her much since everything happened. "He's got shit going on, Charlie. He doesn't have time to deal with this. He's got practice half the day and he's trying to prove he still belongs there. It would have been a bad idea for me to go."

"That makes sense but he loves you. You're more important

than all of that and you love him too. You guys have been through so much that I just…I don't want you to lose it. Not after everything."

For something to do, I move my cell from one hand to another. "We won't lose anything." We can't. We've fought for each other and suffered without each other. But right now…I'm suffering with him too—when I look at him or talk to him. Then I'm pissed because I love him so damn much. I shouldn't be suffering when I know he wants to be there for me.

A noise catches my attention and I look over to see my mom walking toward me. She's early too. That has to be a good thing.

"She's here. I gotta go, Charlie." After I stand, I shove my phone into my pocket. It's ridiculous that I don't know if I should walk toward my own mom or not—that I'm so nervous to see her.

"Hi." I point toward the table. "Wanna sit?"

"Sure." She smiles, that one movement pushing some of my fear away. Mom sits and then I sit down beside her.

"So…I'm guessing Dad told you." I'm looking at my hands instead of her, which is ridiculous. Shoving them under the table, I turn, my eyes on her.

"Of course he did, Alec. I'm…shocked to say the least. I don't understand, to be honest. How could we have never known? You never gave any indications that you could be…"

"Gay?" I finish for her.

"Yes. You know I don't have any problem with the gays. They can live their life and I'll live mine. But you're my son, Alec. This is different. I don't understand. We didn't raise you like this. You've been living with that boy all summer and you're suddenly gay?"

I shuffle my feet, trying not to walk away. Tighten my hands into fists because I'm not sure what else to do. If I focus on that, I don't have to concentrate on how I feel.

"You don't raise people to be gay or not, Mom, and Brand didn't turn me that way either. I've...I've been in love with him in one way or another since I was fifteen."

She doesn't reply, only chews her bottom lip, which she does when she's nervous.

"You said 'but you're my son.' Doesn't that mean it shouldn't matter? That you'll love me regardless?"

Her eyes flash with worry, or confusion. I can't tell which. "Of course I'll always love you. That's never going to change."

My lips start to stretch into a smile. My chest suddenly feeling lighter. But the way her eyes dart down, dart away from me tells me loving me doesn't matter.

"It's just going to take some getting used to, Alec. Your father and I just need to make sense of things. Are you going to be with Brandon? Your dad said you were going to move away with him. A lot of people won't understand. I'm trying but I don't either."

"What's there to understand? I've known I was gay since I was young. I tried to hide it because of Dad. I thought I could make it go away...but I can't. And I don't want to either. It's who I am."

"But if you pushed it aside for all these years...I know you used to care for Charlie."

There's my answer right there. She doesn't understand, or she doesn't want to. I told her it's who I am and she wants me to hide it. I take a deep breath and stand.

"I thought I could pretend with Charlie. I don't want to lie about who I am anymore. Why is it wrong to love someone?"

Mom pushes to her feet too. "It's not. That's not what I'm saying, Alec. Like I said...we just need some time. Maybe one day..."

Maybe one day... That's all I need to hear. Why should I have to wait? Wait for them to get used to me? To decide they love me whether or not I'm gay? That I'm okay or that there isn't anything wrong with me?

"You let me know if that day ever comes, okay? In the meantime, I want you to know there's nothing different about me. I'm the same as I've always been."

When I turn and start to walk away, I listen, wondering if she's going to ask me to stop. She doesn't.

* * *

Charlie calls me twice on my way home but I ignore it both times. Rehashing what went down with Mom doesn't sound fun. I just want to forget it all. For this to not be such a big deal.

As I sit in my truck in the parking lot, I think about calling Brand. I want to call him but I'm pretty sure he's at practice. And for the first time since I've known him, I feel like he wouldn't understand. My heart thumps betrayal at that. I'm betraying him by even thinking it, and I know that.

When I round the corner toward my apartment, I stumble a little when I see who's standing there, leaning against my door.

"I've been waiting for you forever, man." Logan crosses his arms. My first thought is to ask him to go. I don't want to deal with anyone today.

"It didn't go well, did it?" he asks.

"How did you know?"

"Been there, remember?" He picks up a bag at his feet. "I brought beer."

"I'm with Brandon," I say, not sure why I said it.

"I know. But he's not here and you need a friend. We are that, right? I mean, we've been friends for months. That hasn't changed all of a sudden, has it?"

Guilt rumbles through me. I've been feeling that a lot lately. Logan's been a good friend to me and Brandon knows about him. It's not a big deal to have him in.

I unlock the door and Logan goes in. He pulls out two beers and puts the rest in the fridge. I have half of mine gone before my ass hits the kitchen chair.

"How bad?" He sits across from me.

"Could've been worse. There was hoping I could fake it, blaming Brand and a *maybe* that she could come to terms with it one day."

"Shit, man. I'm sorry."

I shrug. "Like I said, it could have been worse. It's just shitty to lose your family in one week."

"Bastard," Logan mumbles under this breath.

"What do you mean? Who are you talking about?" Though I'm pretty sure I know.

"He shouldn't have left you. Not right now."

I take another drink before setting the bottle down. The last thing I want to do is talk to Logan about Brandon. "He had to go. He didn't have a choice. Plus, he tried to stay. I wouldn't let him, and he wanted me to go."

"Go watch him play straight with his football buddies? Sounds like exactly what you would want to do after your family turned their backs on you for being gay."

I wince because how many times have I thought that the past few days? But then, I never told Brandon. If I did, he would have done whatever he could to make it better for me. *Except being real…*

"I'm probably an asshole for saying this, Alec, but I'm going to do it anyway. Are you sure you can do this? Lose your family for some guy you have to stay in the closet for? You're going to pretend he's your roommate after everything you guys have been through?"

"It's not just him. I put off coming out too. I didn't even choose to do it when it happened." The instinct is there to defend Brandon, like I know he would with me. Despite the truth in Logan's words, I'm not going to let him put Brand down. I know he loves me and that it won't be a secret forever.

"Yeah but you're out with your family now. It doesn't matter how it happened. You lost them because of it. Should it be for nothing?"

"It's not nothing if I love him."

Logan curses and stands. "Is that enough? If so, I don't think you'd be here right now. You wouldn't have to hide with me, Alec. Aren't you tired of hiding?"

Logan doesn't touch his beer. Doesn't say another word. Only walks out of my apartment, slamming the door behind him.

No matter how much I try, I can't evict one question from my mind: *Is that enough?*

Chapter 28

Brandon

"Three point nine seven! You fucking beat your best time in the forty! How the hell did you do that?" Donny yells at me like I'm not standing three feet away from him. Dev and Theo are there too.

"I don't know." I shake my head, still trying to wrap my mind around it. To a lot of people, this wouldn't be a big deal. To me it's huge.

And these aren't the people I want to be talking to about it. "It was just once. Who knows if it'll happen again. Listen, I gotta go make a phone call real quick."

"Oh shit, Chase. Are you going to call your girl?" Theo asks.

And in that moment, I don't let myself think. I just let myself say the words that want to come out of my mouth. "No. I'm calling Alec."

"The dude who helped you train?" Dev smiles like he gets it when he's not even fucking close. All I know is I don't want to lie about who I need to share this news with. It might not be everything but it's something.

"I'll catch up with you guys later." Pushing through the locker room doors, I head outside, stopping to lean against the building. I'm sweaty and dirty and haven't showered. There's time for that later though.

As the phone's ringing, a lady in a suit steps up to me. "Number forty-three. You're creating quite the buzz, ya know? The star running back who had heart surgery and only a few months later you're breaking your own records in the forty?"

"Hey." Alec's voice is scratchy, like he'd been sleeping or something.

"Three point nine seven is a good time, Chase. How did it feel?" the woman asks.

I tell her, "Now's not a good time, can we talk later?" While Alec says at the same time, "You beat your own time. I knew you'd do it."

This lady needs to get the hell out of here because I really want to talk him about it. "It was incredible. I wish you were here."

"News travels fast in the sports world. Is that the new girl-friend?" she asks.

"Who are you?" I snap at her.

Alec groans. "I'm gonna let you go."

"No. Don't go. I wanna talk to you. Just...hang on." I look at the woman. "It's not my girlfriend."

Turning, I start to walk away. She starts calling behind me, "We'd love the chance to interview you about everything you've been through. An exclusive. Let me give you my card." I keep walking and she's right behind me. She stuffs her card into my free hand but I don't stop to look at it.

"Shit. I'm sorry. She's pushy as hell. I did it, Al. I did it and I wanted to tell you about it. I wish you would've been here. It wasn't the same without—"

"Your girlfriend?"

My stomach drops at that, and I stop walking. "What? No. I told the guys I was calling you. I didn't tell them I was calling my girlfriend. I don't even know where in the hell she got that."

Alec sighs. "I know. It's just…Things are screwed up right now. I keep taking shit out on you. I don't mean to. There's some stuff I need to sort out, okay? I need you to give me a few days, Brand. You know that fucking kills me to ask you but I need you to give me a little time to get my head on straight."

Every muscle in my body tightens. My heart jackhammers. "What are you saying?" Yeah, it's a stupid question, it's like I'm watching myself—seeing this play out and trying to figure out how we got here. We finally had everything under control and we were together and now this.

"I'm just saying I need a few days. I don't want to screw up and I don't want to do something I'll regret but my head's all fucked up right now. I'll…" He pauses. "We'll talk soon okay? You keep kicking ass out there and we'll talk soon."

Minutes after Alec hangs up the phone, I'm still standing in the same spot, in the middle of the empty parking lot.

* * *

Two days. It's been two full days since Alec and I talked. My body is exhausted but it has nothing on the tiredness of my mind. I've done nothing but work out like crazy. I train hard and practice, run after, lift weights, do whatever I can to try and distract myself.

None of it works.

My apartment is dark except for a small lamp by the couch. My feet won't stop moving as I pace around the living room.

Finally I make myself sit down but it's not long before I'm up again. How the hell did we get here? For years Alec and I played this back-and-forth game. We were together but we weren't. No matter what, we always were there for the other though.

Even when I fucked up and we didn't talk for over a year, I think a part of me always knew he would be there. I damn sure know I would have for him too.

This isn't the same.

My fingers fumble with my cell as I pull it out of my pocket and call Alec. It rings until it goes to his voicemail. After hanging up, I try again, only for him not to answer again.

As if I haven't known since the night we came home from the fight with his dad, I realize I'm losing him. Really fucking losing him.

My hand opens and I drop my phone to the floor. I don't think. Just react, shoving everything off my entertainment center and letting it crash to the floor. "We paid our fucking dues!"

Pacing the room again, I almost trip on the coffee table before kicking it out of the way. My cell there on the floor. I don't know what makes me to do it but I drop down, my back against the side couch and dial.

"We paid our *dues*," are the first words I whisper when Dad answers.

"Brandon? What's wrong? Are you okay?"

I almost hang up the phone, regretting the call, but I can't make myself. When I need someone to talk to, I could always go to Alec. Now, I can't. I just need someone.

"We've been through enough, haven't we? We tried to fight it, and we tried not to tell anyone. We did everything we could. Isn't that enough?" My hands are shaking and my face is wet. I don't even remember the last time I cried. "When is it enough?"

"Slow down, Brandon. It's okay. Did something happen with Alec?" Dad's voice is a mask of calm, trying to hide the tension beneath.

"We just wanna be together. I don't fucking get it. Why it has to be so damn hard just to be together? It shouldn't have to be like this. Why don't we deserve to be happy?" I pull my knees up close to my chest, rest my elbow on one leg, my head resting in my hand. "We paid our dues," I say again. "Isn't that supposed to count for something?"

"Brandon, what happened? Are you still in Ohio? Do you need me to come there?"

"We just wanna be happy. Why can't we be happy?" My hand tightens in my hair. "I don't want to lose him. I don't fucking care about anything else, I don't want to lose him."

Dad sighs. "Then don't, son. You've never let anything else in your life beat you. Don't start now. You were a kid with this crazy dream to play football and I never thought it would happen but it is. You could have died months ago but you're still here. You're not only here, you're out on the field too. You can do anything, Brandon. If anyone can make this work, it's you."

His words don't register. "I'm not as strong as you think. Hell, I don't even know if I want to play ball forever, but I'm too afraid of losing it to tell anyone who Alec really is. I always thought the only thing I was ever good at besides playing, was being with him. I'm not though. I'm not giving him what he needs."

"Brandon," Dad's voice cracks, "you love him. That doesn't mean you're perfect. You love him the best you can. That's all anyone can ask for."

But I'm not. I'm not loving him the best I can. I'm treating him as though there's something wrong with who we are, when there's not.

"And you're good at so many things besides football. Tell me you know that."

My mouth suddenly feels dry. I squeeze the phone tighter. "Am, I? I wasn't good in school. I lied to everyone about who I am. I hurt people. I don't even know what the hell I would do with my life besides ball. It's always been who I am."

"Brandon—"

"There was one time—*once* when I told Mom I didn't know if I wanted to play football anymore. It was the summer she had Joshua. Hell, it was the night she went into early labor because we fought about it. She was mad that I might quit."

"Not because she didn't think you could do anything else, because she didn't want you to lose something you love."

"I don't even know if I love it. I mean, I do, but…" I shake my head, not sure how to make sense of my thoughts.

Dad's cry drifts through the line. The urge to apologize fills me so I can make him feel better. I can't find the words.

"Did we make you believe you weren't more than football?"

"I'm not like you and Nate."

"Brandon, none of us are exactly the same. Not Nate and I or anyone else. Do you realize how strong you are? How much you've accomplished? You've carried this secret with you for so long, son. You shouldn't have had to do that. I didn't see. All these years…I just didn't see. You were the kid I would have dreamt of being when I was young. That's my fault for never telling you that. For never making sure you know how incredible you are and how much we love you. How *good* of a person you are.

"You're loyal, and Christ, we could all learn a lesson from you on how to love. I should have told you that. You were always such a strong, determined kid that I didn't know you needed to hear it. I should have made sure you knew it."

Taking my hand out of my hair, I look forward. "You think so?"

"I know so."

"It felt good...to have something for you to be proud of me about. I didn't have that before football."

"Yes, you did. I am so proud of the person you are, Brandon and it has nothing to do with football. Whatever you decide your mother and I will always believe in you. We will *always* be behind you. There's nothing you can't do."

Those words patch holes and fill empty places inside me. For as long as I can remember, I've needed to hear them. I've always felt sort of weak. I can kick ass on the football field. I can run fast and take hits. I'm the guy people are friends with and want to hang out with but it was always kind of a lie. Just like the rest of my life, it wasn't real because I didn't even have the balls to be honest about who I was. If these people knew who I was, they wouldn't want to be around me. The only thing that wasn't a lie was how I played ball. There was proof and stats and people *wanted* me for that.

But that's not all I want to be. Dad says I'm strong and Alec has always told me I'm more than the guy in my uniform but they were all just words. It doesn't matter if I don't believe it. It's not true if I can't prove it.

"I wanna be the type of guy he needs. The type, *I* need to be. The one who stands up for what he believes in and doesn't hide."

"Then do it, son. I know you can."

And I want that. I want to prove it for him. And I want to prove it for *me*. I've always said I don't know who I am, maybe it's time to start working on being who I want to be. And accepting what I already do know about myself.

"I'm trying, Dad. I'm really trying."

* * *

"Practice kicked fucking ass today! We are going to own it this year!" Dev yells.

"O-hi-o!" Donny adds. "Lancers!"

Everyone is talking and laughing as we stand around the locker room. All their voices are muffled to me, like I'm listening with something plugging my ears. My heart has been going crazy all day and I'm seeing through the same kind of fog that I'm hearing through.

I sit on one of the benches, taking everyone in as they stand around talking. We've all changed already but they're on too big a high to leave yet.

My stomach knots as I ring my hands together, trying to figure out the best way to say it.

How to take that first step toward finding who I am. How can I ever know who that is if I'm not honest?

My vision clears and the plugs fall out of my ears because there is no best way to say it. No way other than just to do it—to take that step to owning who Brandon Chase is. My stomach loosens with the knowledge, this freedom already unlocking me from my chains. I'm going to be me. I *want* to be me. That's all the matters.

I clear my throat, ignoring the pain in my chest. "I'm gay."

A few of the guys close to me stop what they're doing or saying, their eyes falling on me. Louder, so everyone can hear me, I say it again. "I'm gay." More chains are dropping away as the locker room gets quiet around me.

"Are you telling me you're happy, Chase?" Dev asks.

Coach studies me, walking my way. "In my office, forty-three."

"No." I stand. "I'm not going and I'm not telling you I'm happy, Dev. I'm *gay*."

"Um...since when, man?" Theo crosses his arms.

"Since always."

"You're queer?" This from Donny. "What the fuck?"

To my surprise, Dev pushes him.

"No one leave this locker room until we're done talking. Anyone touches their phones and I'm fucking breaking them. You record this, you're off the team, I don't care if I lose my job because of it," Coach growls.

"You're a fag?" Donny repeats.

"Yeah, I'm gay. Got a problem with it?" I take a step closer to him. The locker room is silent, the sound of my pulse a bullhorn in my own ears.

Theo shakes his head. "You gotta admit this came out of nowhere. We're just trying to figure out what the hell you're talking about."

Some of the other guys from the team start whispering in the background.

Each second that I stand here, that I talk, I get lighter. "There's not much to understand. I'm gay. I always have been but...hell, I was too weak to admit it. This is football, man. I'm not stupid. I know how it goes. I'm not lying about it anymore though."

I look at Donny. "Nothing's changed. I'm the same guy I've always been."

"That's bullshit, Chase. You're not the fucking same. If so, you wouldn't be telling us you're a fag."

"You say that again and I'm beating your ass." I step toward Donny, ready to take him out but Coach grabs him.

"I'm not hiding it anymore. It is who I am. I'm also not leaving the team. Nothing's changed. I'm still faster than anyone on the team and I'll kick your ass too. If anyone has a problem, we need to deal with it here."

Theo steps toward me. Damned if that one doesn't hurt. He's cool and I don't want to lose him as a friend.

But then…he holds out his hand. It takes me a minute but then I reach out and grab it.

"I don't give a shit who you fuck, Chase, as long as we win football games. The way I look at it, more girls for me."

A few of the other guys laugh.

Dev pushes my shoulder. "I know I'm good-looking. As long as you can handle being around me and don't go falling in love with me, or something, I'm good, bro." He smiles so I know he's kidding.

I hit him back. "Fuck you. You're not my type. I already have someone anyway."

Theo jumps on the bench. "Ah fuck. Chase has a boyfriend. This whole time I've been giving him shit about being pussy whipped."

I run at him and he jumps down right before I get there. There's more laughing after that and then Coach tells us all to calm down because we have to talk seriously about this. It's not perfect. Donny sits on the other side of the room from me, his arms crossed. A couple other guys are around him, all of them keeping their distance and looking at me like they're ready to kick my ass. But overall, everything is okay. They're assholes and if they can't deal with me, I don't give a shit about them.

Coach comes at the whole thing professionally, asking my plan about coming out and all that and then tells everyone to keep their mouths shut until I say anything. I can tell he isn't sure how to handle the whole situation but he's not bailing on me either.

When everything finally starts to settle down, Theo and Dev come up to me. Automatically I cross my arms, ready to deal with it if they changed their minds.

Theo nods his head. "I just wanted to say sorry. I know I've said shit…not thinking, about people acting gay or you having a boyfriend or whatever. It's just…shit people say. I didn't mean anything by it."

"It's shit people shouldn't say, man."

He nods. "We cool?"

"We're cool."

Dev speaks next, "I have an uncle who's gay. My mom is the only person in her family who talks to him. He's still my uncle and you're still my boy." He holds out his fist and I bump it with mine.

For the first time in my life, I walk out of the locker room… free. Feeling like, *me*.

Pulling my phone out of my pocket, I dial. There's one more thing left to do.

Chapter 29

Alec

When I get out of the shower, I pull on a pair of shorts. I don't feel any better than I did before I went in. It's been two days since Brandon tried to call me last. Since I was an asshole and didn't answer.

I tried twice today but his cell when to voicemail each time.

Not that I know what I plan to say to him anyway. I miss him like hell but I don't know if I can keep hiding anymore either.

On my way down the hall, there's a knock on my front door. I almost go back to my room for a shirt, instead I just keep going.

As soon as I pull the door, Brand walks inside. All I can think is: *Damn, it feels good to see him.* Automatically, my body relaxes from the tension that's gripped it for what feels like forever.

"Come on. We gotta hurry." He grabs my wrist and pulls me into the living room. I hardly have time to close the door.

What the—? "Brand, what are you doing here?"

"I know you said you needed a few days. Technically it's been that." He turns to me, winks, and smiles. It hits me right in the chest. Holy shit is he sexy as hell.

And he's…happy. Different.

"You wanna argue with me but don't. My fucking plane was late and I thought I was going to have to call you and tell you to watch it by yourself. It was like a movie, man. I paid the cab extra to drive like a bat out of hell and everything. And that's *after* I threatened to go somewhere else if it couldn't play when I needed it to and had to beg my coach for a couple days off."

I'm stumbling behind him trying to figure out what the hell he's talking about.

Brandon hits the power button on my TV.

I pull to a stop, making Brand stop too. "What's going on?"

He sighs and steps closer to me. "You'll see. I know things have been screwed up but…trust me. You still trust me, right?" His hands land on my bare sides and he holds me waiting for my answer.

Damn if I don't want to keep his hands on me. To touch him too. "You know I do. It wasn't about that. It's just—"

Brandon leans forward and presses his mouth to mine. The kiss is quick but everything I missed at the same time.

"Shh, baby. Just watch, okay? We'll talk in a minute." Brandon turns it to *College Football Now!* and then he's dragging me to the couch to sit down.

It's not thirty seconds later, I see why. Brandon's on TV, sitting at a desk with a woman across from him. I'm pretty sure my heart stops beating.

"We're here with Ohio Lancers running back, Brandon Chase. I'm sure most of you out there think we're here to talk about his recent injury but that's not why Brandon asked if he could come here today, is it?"

He clears his throat. "No. But I am going back this season. I can promise you that. I'm not going anywhere."

She smiles.

"That's just one of the big things in my life right now though."

"Well, I'll just let you come out and say it then."

It takes Brandon a couple seconds before he looks up and says, "Now that I'm here, it feels kind of crazy to do it like this. To make it such a big deal because it really shouldn't be, should it?"

"What shouldn't be?" she asks him.

Brand shrugs. "Who I love." He scratches his neck. "That I'm gay."

I whip toward him, Brandon already staring at me. He came out. He came out in a huge-ass way. I can't find the words to say any of that though. All I can do is look at him. The urge to touch him hits me again but I can't make myself move.

Brandon nods his head toward the TV. "Watch. You're missing it."

I smile before giving the TV all my attention again. Unable to look away from him, on national TV, being the strongest damn person I know.

Brandon tells her he's hid his sexuality his whole life. That he's known for years. That he was scared of who he was, and scared of how people would react to it. She asks him questions and he answers them all—no fear.

Reaching over, I slide my hand to his inner thigh as I keep watching. She asks him about coming out to his team, which he tells her he did. On, and on, and on. It's crazy, surreal, like some dream that I never thought would happen. So many thoughts ram into my head but I can't sort them out. I don't know what to say.

"Why now, Brandon? What's changed that you decided you need to come out now?" she asks.

I scoot forward to the edge of the couch as though that will somehow make him answer quicker. As though he's not right next to me.

"A few reasons, I guess. Like I said, I've been scared of this my whole life. Scared of people's reactions and worried they'd think how I feel is wrong. But then...well, I guess by my hiding it, it's like I thought it was wrong too. Maybe I did before but I don't anymore. I wanted everyone to know that. To know who I am. The scared guy isn't who I want to be."

He takes a deep breath. "I've been in love with a guy since I was sixteen. We've denied it, hidden it, and broken up. None of that changed how I felt about him. It didn't change the person I was.

"And then we tried to get back together while we were lying to the world about it. Not because of him, because of me. I didn't want to be the gay football player. I didn't even really know who I was. The only time I ever really made sense is when I was with him."

The woman on TV cocks her head, looking at Brandon so sincerely. My body is begging me to do the same thing but I can't turn away from what he's saying either.

On TV, Brandon sighs. "I hurt him. I hurt me. It's not supposed to be that way. Loving each other shouldn't be a crime. I didn't want it to be like that anymore.

"He lost people close to him because of how he feels about me. I just...I guess I wanted to make sure he knows there's nothing to be ashamed of. I'll never be ashamed of him. My whole life I thought my worth lied in how fast I could run or how many yards I could rush. That's not all there is to who I am. There are things—people who are more important than anyone else. He gives me a rush being on the field never can. He makes me feel like someone. I mean, if he can love me, there has to be something there, right? Why would I hide that?"

The woman wipes her eyes. "That was beautiful."

"I was going for sexy." Brand smiles, and she laughs.

From there she goes into the effect on sports and how it's changing with more players coming forward. Picking up the remote, I hit power. When the TV goes off, I drop the remote to the coffee table, still unable to find any words.

"Tell me you thought it was sexy. Hell, I'm going to catch so much shit for that."

He's trying to make me laugh but it doesn't work. I keep hearing his words, the interview in my head and replaying everything that's gone down recently. "I'm sorry."

"What are you sorry for?" Brandon asks.

"For pushing you away. For being a jealous prick because of the things I'd lost, and blaming you for it when it wasn't your fault. For not talking to you about it."

"Hey, I screwed up too. I screwed up more than you have, Al, but we're starting over now, yeah? Plus you were right to be upset. I never should have expected you to hide like that, to pretend to be just my friend. It was wrong. I'm honored to love you and I shouldn't have tried to cover that up."

I get on my knees in front of him, kneeling between Brandon's legs like he did to me not very long ago. Looking up at him, I say, "You're brave as hell, Brand. What you just did was huge." And yes I know he did it for himself but he did it for me too. I know that and it's not something I'll ever forget.

"I was going for sexy," he says again. Brandon sobers then, and asks, "What happened with your mom? I should have asked you that first but I didn't want you to miss it."

That is Brandon. He has such a big damn heart that tried so long to hide behind all that fear.

I take a deep breath, rest my hands on his thighs and he

cups the back of my neck. "Not as bad as dad. She loves me but she can't handle it. Maybe one day she can accept it. Not now though."

"Shit, I'm so sorry. I wish I would have been here with you." He drops his forehead to mine.

"What you did was better." Then I add, "Sexy."

"Finally!"

I can't help but laugh. "I missed you. So fucking much."

"I missed you too, baby." His lips touch mine and his tongue slips into my mouth. Pushing forward, I rise to my feet before coming down on him as he sits on the couch. Brandon's hands run up and down my neck, back, chest and it was just like he said in the interview—it's a rush that I only get from him.

"I know it's not the same and I hope like hell we can work things out with your family but you know you have me, right? I'm yours, Al. You always have me and my family loves you. We can do this. We'll do it right this time and fuck anyone who has a problem with it. Tell me you wanna make this work."

I remember what he's said to me before. "It's not that I don't want to be with you. I just had to work some stuff out. I've always wanted you. You know that. It's our time now, Brand. I don't want to lose you again."

"You won't." His fingers trace my abs.

We've been through so much shit over the years. So much pain and so many lies and fears but being here with him now, honest and together willing to fight anything that stands between us, I know two things.

I love him and I'm not ashamed of that. I don't give a crap who doesn't get it or has a problem with it. We're all that matters and we love each other.

And the second thing is… All the shit we've dealt with—the pain and the anger and the secrets—brought us where we are right now.

And being with him is worth everything we've had to go through.

Epilogue

Brandon

Music blasts through the speakers, echoing out through the room. About seventy-five people wander around. Some of them are dancing, while others are in little groups talking.

Theo and Dev jerk around in the center of the room, doing some fucked-up kind of dancing and making their girlfriends laugh. I lean against the wall in the corner, and take a drink of my beer.

"You just graduated from school this weekend. You're not supposed to be hiding out in the corner." Alec steps up beside me. Reaching out, I touch his blond hair that's a little shorter now than it used to be.

"Maybe I was waiting for my boyfriend to come and find me." I nod my head a little, telling him to come here. Alec steps closer to me as I rest my hand on the back of his neck. "You look sexy."

He rolls his eyes. "What's the difference? I always look sexy."

A laugh tumbles out of my mouth. Setting my beer on the table, I look at him again. The urge doesn't hit me to pull away. It never does anymore. He's mine and I'm his and I want the whole fucking world to know it. Being gay is part of who I am and I'm proud of that. I'm proud of him.

The corners of Alec's blue eyes wrinkle. "What's wrong? You look upset."

"Nope." I shake my head. "Quit pretending like you know everything about me."

Alec chuckles because we both know he does. "Do you regret it? Not going into the draft?"

Most of my friends did. Theo's heading to New York, and Dev to Green Bay. I get asked all the time if I wish I would've gone. Why I decided to throw all that talent away but I don't see it like that. I didn't lose my skill. I just decided there are things more important to me. "You know I don't. Do I wonder what could have been? Sure, I wouldn't be human if I didn't but that's not what I need outta life. There's other things in life other than football." And it was on my terms. Not because I couldn't play ball or because I thought I had to. Not even because I didn't want to be a gay football player. I did it because it's what I want.

"Not if you ask some people."

"I don't care what other people think. Just us." I'd be lying if Alec didn't have a little to do with my decision. Not that he asked me or anything. He wouldn't do that but damn, we've already lost so much time together, I don't want to leave all the time. I don't want to uproot our plans and switch cities, especially when he's still in school.

"Brand…"

"Alec…" I smirk and he shakes his head. We've talked about his a million times but I know he worries. "We don't have to do this. You know me better than anyone. You know I loved football but I never really wanted to live it. It's a part of who I am, not the whole. And yeah, I know going into the NFL wouldn't automatically mean football is who I am but I just...you know I have other things I want to do now. Important things that make me feel good...that make me feel like *me*. I didn't know who I was for far too long. Now I do."

"I always knew." Alec leans forward. My hand tightens on the back of his neck, as he fists my shirt and kisses me. My tongue slides between his lips, and I taste *him*. It's familiar and so fucking incredible.

"Fucking hell. Chase is making out with his boyfriend again. I swear you're a horny bastard. Get a room." Theo grabs Alec's shoulders and mine and pretends he's trying to pull us apart.

"You jealous?" I tease him.

"Maybe a little," he replies.

"What?" His girlfriend swats his arm.

"I said only a little. I bet Alec never says he's not in the mood because he has a headache."

Everyone laughs, even Theo's girl.

"You're an idiot," Dev tells him.

"Don't pretend you never thought of it, man." Theo nudges Dev.

Theo and Dev are the only guys from the team I really talk to anymore. It's not that most of them aren't cool with me being gay. They are but things are different with them. They're more than just teammates, they're friends. Not just to me but to Alec too. Donny and I haven't talked since the season ended. It sucks but what are you gonna do? I don't need people like that in my life.

"Your parents throw a pretty kick-ass party." Dev looks around the room Mom and Dad insisted on renting out for a graduation party.

"They're proud of him," Alec adds. I wrap my arm around him.

"How long will you guys stay in town?" Theo's from here so he's not heading to New York right away.

"Only like a week or so," Alec answers. "We're spending the summer in New York. Brand's dad's helping us get the football camp off the ground. There's a lot we have to do before next summer."

"What's it gonna be? Like a two-week program or something?"

"Yeah, either that or a month. Just a day camp though." I don't remember what made the idea come to me but as soon as I'd shared it with Alec he'd been down. We've been talking to my dad about it a lot and he's helping us organize it, since we want to move to New York once Alec graduates.

"That's cool that you guys are doing that."

It was my tutor who turned me onto football. Yeah, the game was never exactly what other people thought it was to me but it gave me confidence too. It made me feel like someone when I was a kid. Now we're hoping we can do the same thing for teens. Let them know that you can be gay and play sports too. Or a really, a place where any teen can come to learn to play. Where they're all accepted.

"Thanks."

We talk to them for a while before they disappear to dance again. Charlie comes over and drags Alec to dance too. I talk with Mom and Dad for a while. Nate and I chase Joshua around and stuff like that before Alec makes his way back to me.

He hands me his cell. There's a text from his mom that says, "Tell Brandon congrats."

His dad never came around but things are okay with his mom. You can tell she's still a little uncomfortable with us being together. Still, she calls him now. We're considering going to see her this summer. And no matter what, he has my family too. They love him like a son, and he'll always have me.

I'm not going to pretend it's not a little awkward talking to her. But she's trying and that counts for something.

"That was cool." I push the cell in Alec's front pocket

He smiles. I know it means a lot to him to at least have his mom in his life.

"I've never danced with you." Alec pulls me to him by a loop of my jeans.

"You just want an excuse to be close to me."

"So?"

"Never said I was complaining."

We hold each other close and move to the music. My hand rubs up and down his back, savoring the feel of his body. "We did it, Al. We really fucking did it." I can't imagine my life without him. Loving Alec helped me decide who I want to be. That's all I ever had to do, was decide who that was. It's always been my choice.

"I know. It's still crazy to think about but we're here."

Together, the way we're supposed to be.

"I love you."

"I love you too, Brand."

You Might Also Like...

Pixie Marshall is hoping that a summer of free room and board working with her aunt at the Willow Inn will help her forget her past. Except there's a problem: the resident handyman is none other than Levi Andrews. The handsome quarterback was once her friend—and maybe more—until everything changed in a life-shattering instant. Levi can't believe he's living with the one person who holds all his painful memories. More than anything he wants to make things right, but a simple "sorry" won't suffice—not when the tragedy that scarred them was his fault. Levi knows Pixie's better off without him, but every part of him screams to touch her, protect her, wrap her in his arms, and kiss away the pain. Yet even though she's so close, Pixie's heart seems more unreachable than ever. Seeing those stunning green eyes again has made one thing perfectly clear—he can't live without her.

Detective Rocki Bangli has spent the past four months under-
cover, trying to get the goods on drug lord Darrell Archer. Now
that she's gained Darrell's trust, he's given her a job: keep an eye
on the Beaumont Body Shop, a car detailer and private investiga-
tion agency. There's only one problem—her target is the hot and
very sexy Tony Weston, whose eyes tell her he's on to her game.
Tony spotted the gorgeous detective a year ago at the police
academy and never forgot her. A thousand fantasies later, he
finds Rocki working for the most dangerous man in town. Now,
Tony's determined to find out what's going on...*after* he brings
her home with him. But when her position is compromised, suddenly Rocki and everyone she loves might be in danger. Now
Rocki must trust Tony with her secrets, her mission, and her
life—or it could be the end for both of them.

Melanie O'Bryan knows life is too short to be afraid of taking chances. And former Air Force sergeant Bennett Hart is certainly worth taking a chance on. He's agreed to help her students with a school project, but she's hoping the handsome handyman will offer her a whole lot more. Yet despite his heated glances and teasing touches, Mel senses there's something holding him back. Bennett Hart is grateful to be alive and back home in Mirabelle, Florida. Peaceful and uncomplicated—that's all he's looking for. Until a spunky, sexy-as-hell teacher turns his life upside down. After one smoldering kiss, Bennett feels like he's falling without a parachute. But with memories of his past threatening to resurface, he'll have to decide whether to keep playing it safe, or take the biggest risk of all.

Workaholic Nick Taziano is the proud owner of a successful marketing company in Montana. But his career takes a backseat when he learns his dad plans to remarry his ex. Nick fears she'll break his heart…again. And he doesn't like being reunited with her obnoxious daughter—until the all grown-up beauty kisses him at the engagement party. The kiss might be a mistake, but once he tastes Jane's lips, nothing—not even her famous blueberry pie—compares. A promising chef at Big Sky Pie, Jane Wilson never, ever wanted to see Nick Taziano again, but he's just been hired to do the pie shop's marketing. How's a girl supposed to bake the best pastries in town when he's a constant reminder of their steamy chemistry? His chocolate eyes and sexy dimples heat up the kitchen—and every part of her body. Jane has no room for a man in her life, yet sometimes the most delicious dishes don't follow the recipe

Both Cheyenne and Colt know life is never easy, but neither of them expect the tragedy that threatens to end their charade and rip them apart forever.

Can love save them?

After her father commits a crime that shatters her family, eighteen-year-old Delaney Cross is tired of pretending everything is alright. Packing up her car, she sets out to find the people her father hurt. Her search leads her to places she's never been—and into the arms of Adrian Westfall.

To the outside world, Adrian is a sexy, charming ladies man. But his playboy persona is just an act. Secretly his soul is tortured by a memory too painful to share. Only Delaney seems to see through his façade to the real man underneath. And for the first time in his life, Adrian feels he can begin to open up about his past.

Together, Adrian and Delaney share a passionate, carefree love they never expected to find. Yet both still harbor their own secrets. When the dark truth is finally revealed, will it bring them closer together, or tear them apart forever?

A biker. A tattoo artist.
A love to last a lifetime.

Maddox Cross has always had to be tough. When his father went to jail for murder, the teenager took care of his sister and mother. Now on his own and working security at a night club, Maddox wants to become a tattoo artist—a dream that comes closer to reality when he falls for the hottest, most tatted woman he's ever seen. She's wild and beautiful, and Maddox will do anything to be with her.

Bee Malone came to town to open up her new tattoo parlor, Masquerade. Since being kidnapped as a young girl, Bee has had trouble getting close to anyone. But when she meets Maddox, she sees that under his hard biker's body is the sensitive soul of an artist. What starts out as a sizzling one-night stand soon becomes so much more.

Bee wants Maddox to join her tattoo business, but letting him into her life means revealing all her most intimate secrets. And as the past begins to intertwine with her present, Bee fears their love may not be as permanent as their ink…

About the Author

From a very young age, Nyrae Dawn dreamed of growing up and writing stories. It always felt as if publication were out of her grasp—one of those things that could never happen, so she put her dream on hold.

Nyrae fell in love and married one of her best friends from high school. In 2004 Nyrae, her husband, and their new baby girl made a move from Oregon to Southern California and that's when everything changed. As a stay-at-home mom for the first time, her passion for writing flared to life again.

She hasn't stopped writing ever since.

Nyrae has a love of character-driven stories and emotional journeys. She feels honored to be able to explore those things on a daily basis and get to call it work.

With two incredible daughters, an awesome husband, and days spent writing what she loves, Nyrae considers herself the luckiest girl in the world. She still resides in sunny Southern California, where she loves spending time with her family and sneaking away to the bookstore with her laptop.